THE
ALLEY'S SHADOW

"DARE TO ENTER THE ALLEY. BUT BEWARE—YOU MAY NOT LEAVE THE SAME.

by Garima Wadhera

Copyright © 2025 by *Garima Wadhera*

All rights reserved.

This is a work of nonfiction. All characters and descriptions of events are the product of the author's imagination and any resemblance to actual persons is entirely coincidental. The information in this book expresses the author's views and opinions and does not necessarily represent the views of any organization.

First published June 2025

TABLE OF CONTENTS

DEDICATION

To the lonely alleyways and silent shadows This is for the unheard voices echoing in the dark corners of the mind.

To those battling unseen horrors, struggling to separate illusion from reality— may this story remind you that even in the darkest places, there is truth.

And to Anya, a symbol of clarity within chaos— your gaze changed everything.

Index by Theme & Symbol

ACKNOWLEDGEMENTS

Writing this memoir has been a deeply personal and cathartic journey, and I am immensely grateful to the many individuals who supported me along the way. First and foremost, my heartfelt thanks go to my therapist, Dr. Eleanor Vance, whose unwavering guidance and support provided a crucial framework for my healing and self-discovery. Her expertise and compassion were instrumental in helping me navigate the complex emotional landscape of my past.

I am also indebted to the staff and residents of the Havenwood Shelter, whose resilience and unwavering spirits inspired me every day. Their stories, interwoven with my own, are a testament to the human spirit's remarkable capacity for healing and transformation.

A special thank you to my editor, Sarah Miller, whose insightful feedback and meticulous editing helped shape this narrative. Her dedication and understanding were invaluable.

Finally, I extend my deepest gratitude to my friends and family, whose love and unwavering belief in me provided the foundation upon which I rebuilt my life. Their steadfast support was my lifeline during the darkest hours.

Garima is a dedicated writer and advocate for mental health awareness whose personal experience with mental illness has profoundly shaped their perspective and mission. Through their work with the Havenwood Shelter, Garima has gained invaluable insight into the realities faced by those struggling, fueling their commitment to supporting others on their healing journeys.

Holding diplomas in mental health awareness and health and social care, Garima combines lived experience with clinical knowledge to break down stigma and promote equitable access to quality mental health care for all. Their writing weaves personal narrative with professional understanding, fostering empathy and delivering a powerful message of hope and resilience.

Beyond the written word, Garima actively engages in advocacy efforts, striving to build a more compassionate, inclusive, and supportive world for individuals facing mental health challenges.

A haunting psychological descent into the mind of a predator—and the shadow he can no longer control.

In the heart of a decaying city, a nameless man lives two lives. By day, he is a model of sterile perfection—every move calculated, every calorie counted. By night, he becomes something else entirely: a puppeteer in an alley of secrets, weaving rituals of roses, feathers, and shadows to lure the lonely and the broken.

But as the line between control and chaos dissolves, the stage he once ruled begins to turn on him. Victims' eyes linger too long. A misplaced feather disrupts the illusion. The rituals lose their power. And in the stillness, guilt begins to speak.

The Alley's Shadow is a psychological horror novel that explores the terrifying beauty of control—and the horror of its unraveling.

CHAPTER 1

THE SHADOW OF THE ALLEY

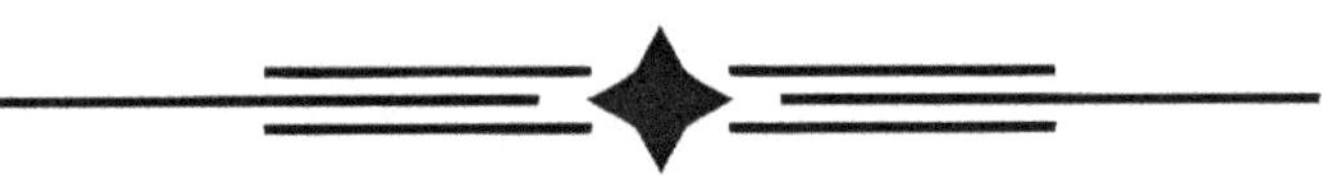

The fridge hummed, a relentless drone against the flat's silence. It was 7:17 A.M. sharp. No alarm was needed; his body, a clockwork marvel, woke precisely. But the nights? Chaos reigned. This daily routine is a gilded cage. It is a meticulously crafted performance every morning: shower, perfect hair, clothes screaming bland competence. Breakfast: one slice of whole-wheat toast, avocado, exactly 200 calories.

Day and night are two starkly different worlds. The day is the act, the carefully constructed lie. The night is the shadow, the horrifying truth, hidden in the alley.

That alley is a character in itself. Grimy brick, whispering secrets. A maze of shadows, the city's festering underbelly. The air hung thick with dampness, garbage, and something else, something wicked, clinging to the back of his throat. Flickering gaslights painted grotesque shadows; the alley seemed to breathe, to twist and writhe. The routine was a lifeline and a prison. He rose with the sun, clinging to the structure, the control. The shower, the grooming, the anonymity – a practiced ritual. The toast, the avocado – a measured beginning. It was his anchor before the storm hit.

He lived a double life, a stark contrast of light and shadow. Publicly, calm and controlled, a mask perfectly in place. But nightfall unleashed him. The alley, a character in itself, its brick walls scarred and secretive, became his sanctuary. Under the dim glow, his true self emerged, shedding the daytime facade.

Even in this grim landscape, a flicker of hope remained. The gaslights, though distorted, offered warmth, a suggestion of possibility. The air, thick with decay and secrets, hinted at change, at transformation. He inhaled it deeply, a potent reminder that anything was possible, even within his rigid routine.

This alley was his domain. Every crack, brick, and rusted fire escape was intimately known. He knew the city's rhythm: sirens, stray dogs, hushed conversations—a symphony of urban decay, his nightly lullaby. The alley was his stage, his theater of shadows.

His nighttime preparations were meticulous, a precise counterpoint to his controlled mornings. Where day was order, night was surrender to the darkness within. Candles flickered, casting eerie shadows; dead roses and crimson tears on the floor served as props; soft feathers, his costume. Every object was chosen and placed with painstaking care. A single misplaced feather, a flame too bright—disaster. The balance was precarious, the act delicate.

These rituals weren't mere theatrics; they were crucial. They guided him through his inner labyrinth, preparing him for the descent into the night. They were incantations, self-hypnosis, severing the ties to his daytime self, allowing the darkness to consume him entirely.

He saw them not as victims but as pawns—each one meticulously chosen, a carefully orchestrated lure into his deadly game. He knew their secrets, weaknesses, and very souls and used this knowledge to manipulate them, to break them. He was the puppeteer; they were his puppets, dancing to his sinister tune.

It wasn't just lust; it was control. Absolute, terrifying control. The thrill? The power. The exquisite pleasure of bending another's will to his own. The alley became his stage, each encounter a perfectly choreographed performance of domination. He relished the power, the precision, the cold detachment as he executed his plans. The aftermath? A chilling, intoxicating triumph. The silence, the emptiness – strangely satisfying.

He vividly remembers the first time: the rain-slicked cobblestones, the moonlight, the woman's eyes shifting from fear to something...worse—a fascination with his power. The act was swift and clinical. There was no rage, just cold calculation.

But the cracks appeared. A flicker of defiance here, a hesitation there. His perfect performance began to unravel. The precision, once flawless, faltered. His control, once absolute, slipped. The ritual, once sacred, lost its meaning. The storm was brewing. His carefully constructed world was crumbling. The game was changing. And he knew, with a sickening dread, that he was losing.

His haven, his stage, the alley, felt wrong. The shadows were thicker, the darkness heavier, like the stones whispered danger. The city's usual sounds – sirens, traffic – weren't soothing anymore; they fueled his growing dread. His whole world, so carefully built, was crumbling. The double life he'd crafted was cracking wide open. This wasn't a game. It was terrifying, far more real than he'd ever known.

Something was coming—a vast, chaotic mess, a showdown shattering everything he'd built. The stage was set, the climax was near, and the curtain was about to fall. He was trapped.

The candles, seven of them precisely, were arranged in a semicircle on the damp concrete.

Not just any candles; these were thick, black tapers, their waxy surfaces

slick with an unnatural sheen. I'd bought them from a shop down by the docks, a place that smelled of salt and decay, a fitting atmosphere for procuring such implements of my nocturnal ritual. Each candle represented something: a past trauma, a suppressed memory, a facet of the fractured self I revealed only under the cover of darkness. Their flickering flames cast a macabre dance of light and shadow across the alley walls, transforming the grimy brick into a canvas of shifting patterns, a surreal backdrop to my twisted performance.

Next came the roses, a dozen of them, each a morbid testament to the lives extinguished. They weren't fresh, vibrant blossoms; oh no, these were meticulously selected, withered, their petals shrivelled and dark, almost black, their once crimson colour now a bruised, decaying purple. I had collected them over several days, carefully selecting those that showed signs of decay, of impending death, a reflection of my internal state. The scent, a faint, sweet rot, hung in the air, mingling with the usual miasma of the alley, creating a cloying, nauseating perfume. They were arranged loosely, scattered amongst the candles, their fallen petals creating a macabre carpet at the heart of my improvised stage.

Finally, the feathers. These were different. Not the coarse, common feathers, but delicate, almost ethereal plumes collected from various sources – a discarded peacock feather from a nearby park, a few soft down feathers pilfered from a discarded pillow I'd found in a dumpster. These were meticulously placed, each a carefully considered brushstroke in my dark tableau. One was placed near a particularly jagged crack in the pavement, another delicately balanced atop a decaying rose, and another nestled in the hollow of a loose brick. They were symbols of fragility, of fleeting beauty, of the inherent vulnerability that drew my victims to me. The soft down against my skin sent a strange, unsettling shiver up my spine – a perverse kind of comfort. Their ethereal lightness contrasted sharply with the harsh reality of what was to come.

The preparation was as crucial as the act itself. It was a meticulous dance, a

self-imposed ritual, a form of self-hypnosis designed to blur the lines between reality and fantasy. The bridge carried me from the carefully constructed facade of myfaçademe existence into the abyss of my nocturnal self. The candles, the roses, and the feathers were not just props; they were totems, talismans, a means of summoning the shadow self that lay dormant within. Without these rituals, the transformation would be incomplete, the act impossible.

I remember one victim in particular, a young man with eyes that held a hint of melancholy. I learned he was a writer and a poet who frequented a nearby bookstore. I had followed him for weeks, observing his habits, vulnerabilities, and the subtle tremors of loneliness that occasionally flickered across his face. His vulnerability was his allure.

He arrived precisely at 11:17 P.M., just as I had predicted. He paused at the entrance to the alley, a shadow lingering at the edge of the streetlight's reach, then hesitated. His eyes fell on the candles, their flickering light dancing in the darkness. A slight tremor ran through his shoulders, a subtle shudder that spoke volumes. He seemed mesmerised, captivated by the scene and my creation's morbid artistry. He stepped into the circle of light, and the transformation was complete.

The encounter wasn't brutal. It wasn't fueled by rage or hatred. It was a precise choreography, a grim ballet played out in the dim light of the alley. The feathers scattered as I moved, the candles casting long, distorted shadows on his face. The scent of decaying roses filled the air. He didn't fight back. He seemed almost willingly subdued, perhaps entranced by the performance. This fueled me—the absolute control, manipulation, and power to orchestrate another's fate.

Afterwards, the emptiness was profound. The alley, once my stage, felt cold and desolate. The scattered feathers and wilted roses were remnants of an increasingly hollow performance. The ritual, once comforting, now felt sterile and incomplete. The euphoria of control was fading, replaced by a chilling void. The whispers of doubt, once barely audible, were growing into a cacophony of self-recrimination. The meticulously crafted delusion was cracking at the seams. The game, once so exhilarating, now felt empty and cruel.

The faces of my victims were beginning to haunt me – not in vivid detail, but as blurred impressions, fragments of memories that clung to the edges of consciousness. Their eyes, filled with fear and fascination, stared back at me from the depths of my mind, their silent accusations a persistent, growing undercurrent. The faces that had once been masked in my theatrical production now seemed to have distinct stories and personalities.

The meticulous planning, rituals, and careful selection of props were no longer a source of comfort but a testament to the insidious nature of my affliction. Each meticulously placed feather, each carefully positioned candle, and each withered rose became a stark reminder of the growing chasm between fantasy and reality. The line was becoming increasingly blurred, almost imperceptible. The comfortable distance I

had maintained between my meticulously constructed fantasy and the brutal reality of my actions was shrinking.

The alley itself started to change, or perhaps it was me

who was changing, my perception distorted by the weight of my actions. The shadows seemed deeper, the darkness more oppressive, as if the walls were closing in. The sounds of the city – once a comforting lullaby – now felt menacing, each distant siren wail a harbinger of doom. The familiar scents of decay and dampness were tainted by something else, a metallic tang that clung to the back of my throat, a constant reminder of the bloodshed under cover of darkness. The alley wasn't just my stage anymore. It was a prison of my own making.

One night, I noticed a discrepancy as I prepared for my ritual. A single feather was missing, usually placed atop a specific withered rose. It felt insignificant at first, a mere oversight. But the absence of that feather set off a chain reaction in my mind. The subtle imperfection disrupted the carefully constructed equilibrium of my world, triggering a cascade of anxieties. Once an integral part of my process, the rituals now seemed empty gestures, a feeble attempt to maintain control in a rapidly slipping world.

My mind, once a meticulously organised theatre, was starting to resemble a chaotic junkyard scattered with broken props and shattered illusions. The shadows were no longer my allies but menacing entities that writhed and shifted in the corners of my vision. The comforting darkness that had once enveloped me was now a claustrophobic blanket, stifling, suffocating, threatening to consume me entirely. My grip on reality was loosening, with every fibre telling me it was slipping from my grasp. The games, elaborate Performances, and meticulous rituals were no longer enough. My meticulously constructed reality was collapsing around me, and there was nothing left to do but watch as the carefully constructed façades of my life came crashing down. The shadow of the alley was becoming my shadow self, and the roles of predator and prey were no longer as clearly defined. The stage was set for a very different kind of performance, a performance where I was no longerincontrol.

The power. That's what it was all about, wasn't it? The absolute, intoxicating power to manipulate, control, and orchestrate another's fate. It wasn't simply about the act itself, the fleeting gratification of the physical. No, it was far more intricate, a complex dance of psychological manipulation, a meticulously crafted game played out in the shadows of the alley. I was the puppeteer, and they, my unsuspecting marionettes, danced to my tune.

Each victim was a carefully chosen piece on my morbid

chessboard. I studied them for weeks, sometimes months, observing their routines, vulnerabilities, and subtle cracks in their armour. Loneliness, insecurity, and a desperate yearning for connection were the chinks in their defences, the weaknesses I exploited with cold precision. I wove intricate webs of deception, subtly manipulating their circumstances and leading them, almost willingly, to their doom. I remember one woman, an artist with haunted eyes and a melancholic smile. She frequented a small, dimly lit café near my apartment, always sitting alone, sketching in a worn leather-bound notebook. I watched her for weeks, studying her habits, expressions, and subtle shifts in her demeanour. She was a creature of habit, predictable in her routines yet simultaneously elusive in her inner world. That unpredictability, that hidden depth, was what drew me to her.

My approach was always gradual and insidious. Started with seemingly innocuous gestures – a dropped book, a chance encounter, a seemingly accidental brush of hands. Then, I'd leave small tokens near her usual table: a single crimson rose, a delicately crafted feather, a poem written on a scrap of paper, its words filled with a potent mixture of longing and despair, words that mirrored her own hidden emotions, words that resonated with her unspoken desires.

Each offering was a carefully calibrated step, a subtle nudge toward the alley, toward the heart of my macabre theatre.

The alley itself was transformed, not merely through the props I placed within it but through my mind, my warped perception of reality. It wasn't just a dark, grimy passageway; it became a stage, my personal theatre, where I controlled every performance aspect. Instead of being oppressive, the darkness became my ally, a cloak that masked my identity and allowed me to assume my role as director and performer. The candles, the roses, and the feathers weren't merely props; they were symbols, totems that helped me maintain my precarious grasp on reality. They were anchors in the swirling chaos of my mind, serving as a bridge between my carefully constructed façade of normalcy and the dark, unsettling abyss of my nocturnal self. The flickering candlelight created an ethereal glow, bathing the alley in a surreal light, transforming thegrimywallsinto a canvas for my twisted fantasies.

The roses withered and decayed, representing the fragility of life and the ephemeral nature of beauty. They were a mirror to my internal state, reflecting the decay and corruption that festered within me. Their scent, a cloying blend of sweetness androt,hung heavy in the air, a macabre perfume that added to the atmosphere.

The feathers were different. Delicate, almost ethereal, they were symbols of vulnerability, of the fleeting beauty I craved and simultaneously destroyed. The contrast between their fragile nature and the brutality of my actions was a significant part of the perverse allure of my ritual. They scattered across the ground as a reminder of the fragility of my victims and the fleetingnatureofmyown.

The manipulation was a complex interplay of subtle gestures, insinuations, and carefully chosen words. I never forced anyone; they always came willingly, drawn in by my performance, by the lure of my carefully constructed fantasies. It wasn't about physical dominance; it was about mental control, twisting their perceptions, leading them down a path of their own making. They were complicit, entranced by my meticulous artistry, even if they were unaware of it. There was a perverse satisfaction in watching their surrender, their gradual descent into my carefully woven trap. Their fear, their confusion, their desperate pleas — these were all notes in my symphony of control. The power was intoxicating, a drug that fueled my obsession, blurring the lines between fantasy and reality.

But the high was always fleeting, the emptiness profound. The aftermath left me with a chilling sense of void, a hollow echo in the silence of the alley. The scattered feathers and decaying roses were stark reminders of my actions, tangible evidence of the destruction I had wrought. The exhilaration faded, replaced by a growing sense of unease, a creeping dread that whispered of the consequences of my actions.

The faces of my victims, once blurred impressions, began to solidify in my mind, their eyes filled with a mixture of terror and haunting recognition. Their silent accusations echoed in the recesses of my mind, growing louder, more insistent, a constant reminder of the lives I had extinguished. The game, once a source of perverse pleasure, now felt cruel, hollow, and increasingly meaningless.

The meticulous planning and elaborate rituals were no longer sources of comfort but rather a testament to the insidious nature of my delusion, a stark reminder of the growing chasm between my perception of reality and the actual consequences of my actions. The delicate balance between fantasy and reality writhed, threatening to engulf me. The alley's darkness was no longer a stage but a prison of my own making.

The control I craved, the power I sought — it was an illusion, a fleeting mirage that evaporated in the cold, harsh light of morning. The emptiness was a gnawing void, a constant reminder of the devastation I had caused. The game of power, once so intoxicating, had become a terrifying reflection of my fractured psyche, achilling

testament to the destructive consequences of untreated mental illness. The thin line between fantasy and reality had shattered, leaving me adrift in a sea of guilt, confusion, and mounting dread, the walls of my carefully constructed world closing in, threatening to crush me under their weight. The shadows of the alley were no longer just shadows; they were the dark projections of my soul. And I was finally beginning to see myself for what I truly was — a monster in my own right.

Her name was Anya. Anya Petrova. I remember the precise cadence of her name, the way it rolled off my tongue, a melody of death. She was a sculptor, her hands — those delicate, artist's hands — capable of moulding clay into breathtaking forms. Ironically, they were also remarkably adept at holding a paintbrush, her canvases teeming with vibrant, almost unsettling portraits. The disturbing part was the eyes — always vacant, empty pools reflecting a deep, internal sorrow that mirrored my own.

I first saw her at the "Blue Moon," a café on a quiet side street, a haven for artists and lonely souls. Anya was a regular, always occupying the same corner table, illuminated by the soft glow of a single lamp. She was a creature of habit, her routine as predictable as the sunrise. This predictability, this almost mechanical adherence to her daily ritual, became the foundation of my plan. It wasn't just about her predictability; her solitude and palpable loneliness were captivating.

For weeks, I watched her. I studied her from across the room, my presence masked by the café's smooth, softly lit ambience, and the murmur of conversations provided the perfect cover for my observation. I devoured every detail: how she stirred her coffee, the tilt of her head as she lost herself in her sketchbook, and the melancholic sigh that escaped her lips regularly. I memorised the pattern of her movements, noting her arrival and departure time and the precise route she took to the bus stop.My initial interactions were carefully orchestrated, innocuous gestures designed to establish a connection without revealing my true intentions. A misplaced book, its cover falling open to a particularly poignant poem. A subtle brush of hands, an accidental bump, left her slightly startled but undeniably aware of my presence. These were the building blocks of our relationship, the carefully laid foundations of her inevitable downfall.

Then came the gifts. Small, insignificant tokens were left anonymously near her table. A single crimson rose, its velvety petals starkly contrasting the rough wooden surface. A delicate grey feather, its lightness a mirror to her fragile emotional state. Each gift was accompanied by a poem written in elegant script, imbued with themes of loneliness and longing. Words that echoed her silent inner world, words carefully chosen to draw her closer to the precipice. The poems were my masterpieces. They were more than just verse; they were carefully crafted psychological probes to exploit her vulnerabilities. They spoke of hidden desires, unspoken yearnings, and deep loneliness that she unknowingly shared with me. They were emotional mirrors, reflecting her inner world in a comforting and subtly manipulative The words were like a siren's call, drawing her ever closer to my trap, to the dimly lit alleyway that served as the stage for my twisted performance. I had chosen it carefully—a secluded passage hidden from view, bathed in an almost theatrical darkness. It became my sanctuary, my stage, where my meticulously constructed fantasies could unfold. She started responding to my advances, albeit subtly. A lingering gaze, a hesitant smile, a barely perceptible nod of acknowledgement. It was a slow, insidious seduction, a psychological dance that played out over weeks, not days. The thrill of the chase, of the slow, deliberate manipulation, was far more intoxicating than the physical act itself.

The night of the encounter was cold and damp. The alley was shrouded in darkness, the only illumination coming from a single, flickering candle I had placed near the entrance. The air was thick with the scent of decaying roses, their wilted petals scattered across the damp pavement. The contrast between the decaying beauty and the stark brutality to come was exquisite.

Anya arrived precisely as I predicted, drawn in by the carefully crafted spell. Her eyes were wide, reflecting the flickering candlelight, her face pale and drawn. She did not appear fearful; she seemed curious, almost expectant. There was a strange resignation in her demeanour, a sense of fatalistic acceptance that filled me with perverse satisfaction. The encounter itself was a carefully orchestrated performance.

It was about control, not brute force. It was about psychological dominance, about twisting her perceptions, about leading her down a path of her own making. Compliance wasn't coerced; it was a willing surrender, an acquiescence to my meticulously constructed narrative.

There was an odd sense of calm in the aftermath, a strange, detached satisfaction. I meticulously cleaned the scene, leaving only the faintest traces—the decaying roses and a single grey feather. The alley, once the stage for my twisted play, was empty and silent.

Only the shadow remained, and it was mine.

The emptiness that followed was profound but different from the one that had plagued me. This was the emptiness of accomplishment, of absolute control. The fear and guilt would come later, but for now, there was only the chilling satisfaction of a meticulously executed plan. The vacant stare of Anya's final portrait, one I had watched her paint weeks prior, haunted my mind, her hollow eyes mirroring my quiet triumph. The game had begun, and I had won the first round. The alley remained my sanctuary, my stage, where the shadows would continue to dance, and the macabre symphony of my mind would forever echo. The next victim was already in my sights, her vulnerabilities meticulously mapped out in the dark recesses of my mind. The game was far from over.

The rain had stopped, but the damp chill clung to the alley, seeping into my bones despite the thick wool of my coat. Anya's absence didn't feel like a void, not initially. It was more like a... stillness. The silence was unnerving, different from the usual urban hum that permeated even the city's most secluded corners. This silence was heavy, pregnant with an unspoken truth. The decaying roses, their scent now diluted by the rain, seemed to mock my victory.

I meticulously wiped down the knife, the steel gleaming under the weak light filtering from a nearby streetlamp. The act felt almost ritualistic, a perverse cleansing that did little to alleviate the unsettling prickle of unease that began to crawl beneath my skin. It was a feeling I had not anticipated, a dissonance in the symphony of my meticulously orchestrated plan.

It wasn't the physical act that troubled me. The control, the absolute dominance, had been intoxicating. It was a subtle crack in the perfect façade of my carefully constructed reality. It was an almost insignificant detail, but it resonated with a disconcerting power.

Anya's eyes. As she'd succumbed, a flicker, a fleeting moment of... surprise? It had been so brief, so quickly overshadowed by the planned resignation, that I almost dismissed it as a trick of the light. Yet it lingered, a ghost at the periphery of my memory. It wasn't fear I had seen, not the terror I expected, but something... different—an unexpected, almost inquisitive curiosity in the face of impending doom.

It wasn't the look of a terrified victim; it was the look of someone who had seen something more, something beyond the carefully constructed narrative I had woven for her. Had she sensed something amiss? A hesitation, a subtle incongruity in my performance? The thought gnawed at the edges of my composure.

The poems, my carefully crafted psychological tools, had worked flawlessly. They had exposed her vulnerabilities and deep-seated loneliness. They mirrored her desires and insecurities with unnerving precision, pulling her into my web with seductive precision. But that momentary flicker of surprise, the final glance, suggested a different story, a narrative that hadn't been written.

The thought fueled a growing unease, a creeping doubt that threatened to unravel the meticulously woven fabric of my control. It wasn't a fear of exposure, not yet. It was a far more insidious fear—that my masterpiece, my perfectly orchestrated psychological manipulation, might have contained a flaw—a flaw I hadn't anticipated, a variable I hadn't factored into my equation.

In the aftermath of the encounter, I meticulously cleaned the scene, erasing every trace of my presence. However, the cleaning, usually a soothing ritual, offered little solace this time. The lingering smell of decaying roses and the single grey feather, reminders of my triumph, now felt like accusations, whispers of doubt echoing in the silence.

Sleep offered little respite. Anya's eyes haunted my dreams, their vacant stare now imbued with an unsettling intelligence, a knowing that chilled me to the bone. The quiet satisfaction I had felt earlier was replaced by a persistent hum of unease, a dissonant note in the symphony of my carefully constructed reality. The control, once absolute, now felt precarious and fragile.

I started examining my methods, replaying the encounter, and dissecting every word and gesture. I had prided myself on my ability to understand human psychology and predict behaviour with chilling accuracy. But Anya's final look suggested a level of perception I had underestimated, a capacity for insight that challenged my carefully constructed theory.

The meticulously mapped-out vulnerabilities of my next target, Sarah, a young woman, seemed less confident. The lines between her insecurities and her actual motivations seemed less apparent, blurred by the nagging doubt that Anya had planted. The precision, the cold calculation that had once defined my methods, now felt... imprecise.

I questioned my choices, analysing the nuances of manipulation and the delicate dance between control and perception. The certainty that had once characterised my approach began to erode, replaced by a gnawing uncertainty. The shadows in the alley, once my companions, now seemed to hold a sinister intelligence, their darkness reflecting the turmoil within me.

The meticulous planning, the carefully constructed narratives, the flawless execution—it all felt different now, tainted by the seed of doubt. It was a subtle shift, barely perceptible to the casual observer, but a seismic event. The carefully crafted edifice of my control was cracking, the foundation of my world beginning to crumble. The ensuing weeks were a blur of obsessive self-analysis and increasingly erratic behaviour. I repeatedly replayed Anya's final moments, searching for answers, for a key to unlock the mystery of her unexpected gaze. My sleep grew restless, filled with nightmares of hollow eyes and accusing whispers.

My usual routine disintegrated. A new element—uncertainty—disrupted the precise, almost robotic order that governed my life. I made impulsive decisions, breaking my established patterns, an apparent deviation from my meticulously planned lifestyle. This was uncharacteristic, starkly contrasting the controlled precision that had always been my hallmark.

The change was subtle, almost imperceptible, but there was a slight tremor in the carefully constructed façade I presented to the world. It was a warning sign that the carefully built control I had meticulously cultivated was starting to fracture. The cracks were tiny, barely visible, but they spread, threatening to shatter the illusion I had carefully maintained.

The subtle change in my behaviour, the erratic shifts in my routine, and the haunting memory of Anya's unexpected expression were the seeds of doubt, the first cracks in the impervious armour I had donned. They were harbingers of the impending storm, the prelude to the eventual collapse of my carefully constructed world. The game was far from over, but the rules had changed. The shadows in the alley were no longer my allies but silent witnesses to my inevitable downfall. And the fear, once a distant possibility, was now a tangible, terrifying presence. The carefully constructed walls of my control were beginning to crumble. The symphony of my twisted mind was starting to lose its harmony, and the discordant notes of uncertainty threatened to drown out the carefully orchestrated tune of my dark design.

CHAPTER 2

THE UNRAVELLING

The alley felt different now. It wasn't just the lingering chill or the stench of decay; it was a palpable shift in the atmosphere, a thickening of the shadows that seemed to press in on me, mirroring the suffocating pressure building within my mind. The rain had returned, a relentless drumming against the grimy brick walls—a soundtrack to the chaos unfolding within me. Before, the alley had been a stage, a backdrop for my carefully orchestrated performances. Now, it felt like a cage, its walls closing in, reflecting the claustrophobia that had become my constant companion.

Once precise and calculated, my actions were now driven by an unsettling urgency. The interval between targets had shrunk, the meticulous planning replaced by a desperate need to act, to prove something—even to myself. Sarah, my next victim, was not a carefully chosen pawn in a grand game; she was a frantic attempt to reaffirm my control, to silence the growing dissonance within. The poems, once instruments of seduction and manipulation, felt clumsy and inadequate, their carefully crafted verses now echoing with the hollow ring of my own uncertainty.

The meticulous grooming, the hours spent studying her routines, the crafting of the perfect psychological profile—it all felt rushed and haphazard. I skipped steps, neglecting details that once would have been sacrosanct. The obsessive precision that had defined my past actions was replaced by a frantic energy, a desperate need to fill the void that Anya's unexpected gaze had created.

Unlike Anya's fleeting surprise, Sarah's fear was exactly what I had anticipated. It was a predictable response, a confirmation of my power, but it offered no solace, no sense of completion. It was a hollow victory, a fleeting moment of control in a world rapidly spiralling out of my grasp. The satisfaction, once profound and long-lasting, was now fleeting, replaced by an almost immediate return of the gnawing unease.

The clean-up was rushed and sloppy. I left traces—evidence I would have meticulously erased in the past. The act of cleaning, once a ritualistic balm, now felt like a futile attempt to scrub away the stain of my own unravelling mind. Once a silent accomplice, the alley seemed to mock my carelessness with its echoing silence.

Sleep became a battleground. Anya's eyes, those unsettlingly intelligent eyes, haunted my dreams, transforming into a kaleidoscope of accusing faces. The nightmares were more vivid, the whispers more insistent, the sense of impending doom overwhelming. The clarity of thought, the razor-sharp focus that had been my defining characteristic, began to fracture, replaced by periods of disorientation and confusion.

My days blurred into a chaotic dance between meticulous preparation and impulsive outbursts. The carefully constructed façade I presented to the world—the successful professional, the outwardly composed individual—began to crack under the strain. Small inconsistencies crept in, minor deviations from my established routines that only I noticed but which spoke volumes about the internal turmoil consuming me. I became increasingly irritable, prone to outbursts of anger and frustration that were completely uncharacteristic.

The once-orderly structure of my life crumbled. My apartment, once a sanctuary of meticulous organisation, descended into disarray. Books lay scattered, papers piled haphazardly, the once-immaculate surfaces now covered with dust and neglect. The meticulous routines that had governed my life were abandoned, replaced by a chaotic existence driven by impulses I could no longer control.

My social interactions became strained, my carefully crafted persona faltering. I became withdrawn, isolating myself from the few people I had allowed into my life. The careful masks I wore in public cracked, revealing the simmering chaos beneath. The carefully measured responses, the calculated silences, were replaced by erratic behaviour, abrupt changes in mood, and a growing inability to engage in meaningful conversation.

The increasing frequency of my acts of violence, the escalating intensity of the psychological manipulation, became a desperate attempt to regain control—to silence the voices that were growing louder within me. Each act, however, only served to amplify the internal turmoil, each victim a fleeting distraction from the inexorable descent into madness.

The alley became a reflection of my internal state, a dark and menacing space mirroring the oppressive weight of my deteriorating mental health. The shadows, once my allies, now seemed to conspire against me, their darkness an ominous foreshadowing of my inevitable collapse. The chilling rain was now a constant torment, mimicking the relentless torrent of self-doubt and despair flooding my mind. The once-familiar scent of decaying roses, once a symbol of my power, now felt like a morbid reminder of my failures, a macabre perfume to my impending doom.

The once-soothed sense of control shattered. The feeling of power I had derived from manipulating others was replaced with a deep and gnawing sense of emptiness. The victory, once intoxicating, now felt hollow and meaningless. Each act of violence, each psychological conquest only intensified the gnawing emptiness within—a stark reminder of the profound loneliness that fuelled my actions.

The escalating acts were not a sign of strength but a desperate cry for help. My attempts to manipulate and control others were not expressions of power but rather desperate pleas to regain a sense of self, to silence the growing cacophony of doubt and despair overwhelming me. The meticulous planning, the precise execution, and the calculated indifference were all elaborate defences against the terrifying realisation of my own psychological fragility.

The meticulous planning that had once been my strength was now a burden, a testament to the profound disconnect between my meticulously constructed persona and the chaotic reality of my deteriorating mental state. The once-precise movements, the carefully calculated words, now felt clumsy, out of sync with the spiralling chaos within. The alley, once a place of calculated action, now felt like a prison, a reflection of the mental confines that trapped me.

The descent was not gradual but a rapid collapse, a catastrophic unravelling. The self-awareness that had once been my manipulation tool was now a weapon turned against me, exposing the fragility of my carefully constructed reality. The echoes of my actions, the lingering evidence of my crimes, became a constant reminder of my own self-destruction, a testament to the dark consequences of untreated mental illness. The once-clear lines between right and wrong, between control and chaos, blurred and disappeared.

Ultimately, all that remained was the relentless rain, the oppressive shadows, and the crushing weight of my unravelling mind. Once under my complete control, the game was lost—overtaken by the relentless force of my self-destruction.

The flickering gaslight cast long, distorted shadows that danced with the rain-slicked pavement, mimicking the erratic rhythm of my own heartbeat. For the first time, the familiar alley felt… wrong, not in the sense of its inherent grime and decay, but in a deeper, more unsettling way. It was as if the very bricks were breathing, exhaling a miasma of fear that clung to me like a second skin. The meticulously crafted illusion of control, the carefully constructed persona I had cultivated for so long, was beginning to crack under the strain. A fleeting moment of doubt, a sliver of fear, pierced the carefully constructed façade. It was a whisper, a barely perceptible tremor in the carefully orchestrated symphony of my existence. But it was enough. Enough to shatter the illusion of invincibility, to expose the fragile underpinnings of my meticulously crafted world. The rain intensified, mirroring the rising tide of unease within me. Each drop was a tiny hammer blow, chipping away at the carefully constructed walls of my sanity.

The precision, the calculated movements, the methodical planning—all of it felt... off. Once a source of grim satisfaction, the ritualistic cleaning felt frantic and incomplete. I found myself leaving traces, insignificant details that would have been painstakingly erased in the past. It was as if a careless hand had taken over, replacing the surgeon's steady precision with the clumsy strokes of a novice.

Sarah's fear had been... predictable. It was a confirmation, I had told myself, a validation—...of my power. But the satisfaction, the intoxicating sense of control, had been fleeting, replaced by a hollow ache, a profound sense of emptiness. The poem, a carefully crafted tool of manipulation, felt like a blunt instrument, its words now echoing with my soul's emptiness. The meticulously crafted psychological profile, once a source of perverse pride, now seemed flawed and incomplete. There were gaps, inconsistencies that I had somehow overlooked, and blind spots in my usually impeccable analysis. It was as if a part of me, a crucial puzzle piece, had gone missing. This wasn't simply a matter of neglecting details; it was a fundamental shift in my perception, blurring the lines between calculated manipulation and impulsive recklessness.

Sleep offered no respite. Anya's eyes, those unsettlingly intelligent eyes, continued to haunt my dreams, morphing into grotesque parodies, accusing faces swirling in a vortex of guilt and self-loathing. The whispers, once barely audible, grew louder, more insistent, their chilling pronouncements weaving into the fabric of my waking hours. The clarity of thought, the razor-sharp focus that had been my defining characteristic, began to fracture, replaced by periods of disorientation and confusion.

The carefully constructed facade I presented to the world began to crumble. Minor inconsistencies, barely perceptible deviations from my established routines, crept into my life. My colleagues noticed my increasing irritability and the sharp edges of my usually controlled demeanour. I became withdrawn, isolating myself and avoiding the few social interactions I had previously allowed myself. The meticulously constructed masks I wore in public cracked, revealing the chaos that simmered beneath the surface.

Once a sanctuary of order and meticulous organisation, my apartment reflected my internal turmoil. Books lay scattered, papers piled in haphazard heaps, the once-immaculate surfaces covered in dust. The meticulous routines that had once governed my existence were abandoned, replaced by a chaotic pattern of impulsive actions and periods of crippling inertia.

The escalating frequency of my acts and the intensity of the psychological manipulation became a desperate, futile attempt to regain control. Each act, however, only served to amplify the internal turmoil, each victim a fleeting distraction from the inexorable descent into madness. Once profound and long-lasting, the satisfaction was reduced to fleeting moments of hollow victory, quickly overshadowed by an overwhelming wave of self-doubt and despair.

The alley, once a silent accomplice, now felt like a prison, its walls closing in on me, mirroring the claustrophobic grip of my deteriorating mental state. The shadows, once my allies, now seemed to conspire against me, their darkness a chilling premonition of my impending collapse. Once a mere backdrop to my actions, the rain became a constant torment, its relentless drumming mimicking the incessant pounding of self-doubt within my skull. The scent of decaying roses, once a morbid symbol of my power, now felt like a macabre perfume, a grim tribute to my impending doom.

My attempts to manipulate and control others were no longer expressions of power but desperate pleas to regain a sense of self, to silence the cacophony of self-doubt that threatened to overwhelm me. The meticulously planned actions, once a source of perverse satisfaction, now felt like a desperate attempt to hold onto a reality that was slipping through my fingers. The meticulously crafted personas I presented to the world were now just fragile shells, barely concealing the crumbling edifice of my sanity.

The clear lines between right and wrong, between control and chaos, blurred and dissolved into a swirling vortex of confusion and despair. The self-awareness that had once served as a tool of manipulation was now a weapon turned against me, exposing the terrifying fragility of my meticulously constructed reality. The echoes of my actions, the lingering evidence of my crimes, became a constant reminder of my own self-destruction, a testament to the consequences of unchecked mental illness.

The descent was not gradual; it was a sudden, catastrophic collapse. The once-clear boundaries of my self-imposed reality shattered, leaving me adrift in a sea of self-doubt and despair. Once under my absolute control, the game was irrevocably lost, swallowed by the relentless tide of my self-destruction. Once a stage for my meticulously crafted performances, the alley became a grim mirror, reflecting the dark abyss of my unravelling mind. The rain continued to fall, a relentless torrent mirroring the unstoppable descent into the chilling depths of my own making. The silence of the alley was broken only by the rhythmic pounding of rain, a relentless soundtrack to the final act of my self-destruction.

The greasy alley reeked of stale beer and something else, something acrid and metallic that clung to the back of my throat. The rain, a constant companion throughout my descent, had intensified, transforming the treacherous pavement into a perilous, glistening black mirror. And then I saw them.

Two figures, silhouetted against the flickering neon sign of a dilapidated bar, emerged from the shadows. They moved with a practised ease and quiet confidence that sent me a jolt of primal fear. The shadows obscured their faces, yet their presence radiated an authority that cut through the fog of my self-induced delusion. They weren't part of my meticulously crafted reality. They were... intruders.

My heart hammered against my ribs, a frantic drumbeat against the relentless rhythm of the rain. My carefully constructed facade, the mask of calm control I had worn for so long, threatened to shatter completely. The meticulously planned scenarios, the psychological manipulations, and the calculated risks seemed absurdly inadequate in the face of this unexpected intrusion.

One of them spoke, his voice low and measured, cutting through the cacophony of the rain and my racing thoughts. The words were simple, yet they carried the weight of an irreversible judgment. I couldn't recall the exact words, only the chilling certainty that my game was over. The carefully constructed narrative I had spun around myself, the intricate web of deceit I had woven, was unravelling before my eyes, exposing the raw, festering wound of my unravelling sanity.

My mind, usually a fortress of meticulous calculation, was besieged by a chaotic storm of emotions. Fear, not the calculated, controlled fear I had induced in others, but a raw, visceral terror that threatened to overwhelm me. Disbelief warred with a sickening recognition: the reality outside my carefully constructed world had finally crashed into my carefully crafted illusion.

The illusion shattered. The world, once a stage for my expertly orchestrated performances, became a terrifying, disorienting labyrinth. The meticulously planned steps, calculated moves, and psychological manipulations were all reduced to clumsy, impulsive actions devoid of purpose, driven solely by desperation.

My attempts to regain control were pathetic and feeble. I tried to speak, to weave a new narrative, to manipulate them as I had manipulated others. The words caught in my throat, a choked whisper lost in the downpour. My body, usually a tool of precise movements, became leaden and unresponsive. The carefully cultivated persona, the mask of unwavering self-assurance, cracked and fell away, exposing the terrified, fragmented person beneath.

The officers moved with a precision that mirrored my own, a chilling reflection of the methods I had employed for so long. They were not simply arresting me; they were dismantling my world, piece by piece, exposing the hollowness at its core. Each question and observation chipped away at the carefully constructed facade, revealing the insidious rot that had festered within.

The rain seemed to mock my helplessness, each drop a relentless hammer blow, pounding against my skull, mirroring the frantic rhythm of my heartbeat. The alley, once my sanctuary, my stage, now felt like a suffocating cage, its walls closing in, trapping me in the grim reality of my actions.

My perception of time was distorted, moments stretching into agonising eternities, punctuated by the sharp, clipped questions of the officers. The world around me seemed to spin, the rain-slicked pavement blurring into an indistinguishable vortex of shadows and light. My carefully cultivated world, the meticulously planned reality I had constructed, dissolved into a kaleidoscope of disorienting fragments. The sharp edges of my controlled demeanour fractured; my carefully constructed control began to crumble and crack. It was a chaotic, terrifying collapse, as abrupt as it was complete. Once a subtle manipulation tool, the whispers were now a cacophony of accusations, a relentless barrage of self-recrimination. Anya's face appeared in my mind's eye, her intelligent gaze piercing through my shattered defences, and then others followed — a montage of horrified expressions, the faces of my victims, now merged into a single, accusing visage.

Each question was a blow not only to my carefully crafted narrative but also to my very sense of self. My meticulously planned defences, the psychological manoeuvres I had employed with such precision, seemed laughable, pathetic. The satisfaction I once derived...from manipulating others, the power that fueled my actions, was replaced by a profound sense of shame and utter helplessness.

The encounter wasn't a confrontation; it was a demolition. The officers weren't simply arresting me; they were systematically dismantling my carefully constructed reality, exposing the fragility and hollowness at its core. They were not merely witnesses but the final act in a tragedy I had written, directed, and played all too well. Only now, the curtain had fallen, and I stood exposed, naked and vulnerable, before the harsh glare of reality.

The meticulously constructed reality of my mind had been shattered, leaving only the echoing emptiness and the chilling awareness of what I had become. The rain continued to fall, washing away the blood and the illusion of power and control, leaving behind only the stark, terrifying truth. The interrogation room was stark and cold, a stark contrast to the meticulously crafted world I had constructed. The fluorescent lights hummed, a monotonous soundtrack to the relentless dismantling of my carefully constructed self. Each question was a blow, chipping away at the carefully constructed persona I had spent so long perfecting. The carefully planned strategies I had deployed with such surgical precision now seemed laughably inadequate in the face of the overwhelming reality.

The lack of control was terrifying. It was a violation, a shattering of the meticulously constructed order that had governed my life. The familiar rituals, the calculated movements, the meticulously crafted personas – all of them had served as a shield against the terrifying abyss within. Now, that shield was gone, exposing me to the full force of my self-loathing.

My carefully constructed arguments and elaborate explanations, which I had rehearsed countless times, crumbled under the weight of their relentless questioning. My words were empty, devoid of the power and control I had previously exerted. Once a tool of manipulation and persuasion, my voice was reduced to a trembling whisper. The carefully constructed narrative, the illusion of control I had spent years building, began unravelling, leaving a sense of profound disorientation and despair.

Each question was a step further into the abyss, each answer confirming my own failure. The neatly packaged psychological profile I had created of Sarah and others, once a source of perverse pride, now seemed hopelessly flawed. Its carefully constructed details revealed chilling incompetence, a deep-seated lack of insight that had escaped my attention, blinded as I was by my own carefully crafted delusions.

The interrogation went on, an agonising dissection of my carefully constructed world. With their unwavering professionalism, the officers systematically exposed the flaws in my logic, the inconsistencies in my stories, and the cracks in my meticulously constructed reality. The meticulously planned actions that had once provided a perverse sense of satisfaction were now laid bare as impulsive acts fueled by a desperate need for control that ultimately spiralled into chaos and self-destruction.

The fluorescent lights flickered, casting grotesque shadows on the walls, mirroring the shifting shapes of my own unravelling sanity. The silence between questions stretched into unbearable eternities, amplifying the relentless pounding of self-doubt within my skull.

The meticulously crafted persona I had presented to the world began to fade, leaving behind a raw, vulnerable core. The game was over. The meticulous planning, carefully calculated moves, and intricate psychological manipulation all led to the chilling realisation that I had lost control and that the carefully constructed world I had created was nothing more than a fragile illusion. The rain outside mirrored my internal state, a relentless, unforgiving torrent that threatened to wash away the very foundation of my being. The meticulously crafted mask had fallen, and all that remained was the terrifying truth: my own unravelling. The descent was complete.

The steel door slammed shut with a finality that echoed the collapse of my meticulously constructed world. The sharp and metallic sound sliced through the lingering echoes of the interrogation, a stark punctuation mark to the end of an era. The air here was different—cold and sterile, devoid of the subtle scents and carefully curated ambience I had cultivated in my own life. This was not a stage; this was a cage.

The fluorescent lights hummed, a relentless, oppressive drone grating on my frayed nerves. The walls were bare, cold concrete, starkly contrasting the richly textured tapestries of my imagined reality. My carefully chosen attire, a symbol of control and power, now felt like a ridiculous costume, a pathetic attempt to maintain a facade that had crumbled under the weight of reality. The crisp lines of my tailored suit mock my current state, a visual reminder of the illusion I had so diligently crafted.

The small metal cot in the corner was a jarring intrusion into the carefully organised space I was accustomed to. The rough, uncomfortable surface was a world away from the plush silk sheets of my own bed, a stark reminder of the utter loss of control I now experienced. Even the simple act of sitting down felt strange, an intrusion upon the meticulously planned choreography of my daily routine, the meticulously planned routine that had been so thoroughly disrupted.

Sleep was a distant memory, a luxury I could no longer afford. My mind raced, replaying the arrest events, dissecting each word and gesture, searching for any flaw in their approach. But there were no flaws. Their efficiency had been as precise, as calculated, as my own – a chilling reflection of the methods I had employed for so long.

The silence of the cell was deafening, a void filled only by the relentless humming of the lights and the relentless pounding of my own thoughts. The silence amplified the inner turmoil, a stark contrast to the controlled chaos I had orchestrated in my life outside. This silence, this enforced solitude, was torture far more effective than any physical restraint.

I tried reconstructing my meticulously crafted narratives to weave new scenarios to regain control. But the words felt hollow, lifeless, devoid of the power and conviction they had once held. My mind, usually a well-oiled machine of manipulation, was stuck, jammed, unable to generate the necessary illusions. The carefully constructed defences and the intricate psychological manipulation layers had collapsed. I was left exposed, vulnerable, bereft of the carefully cultivated armour that had shielded me from the world's harsh realities.

My stomach churned with a mixture of fear, regret, and self-loathing. The hunger pangs were sharp and intense, a brutal reminder of the physical needs I had neglected in my obsessive pursuit of control. The deprivation was more than physical; it was a stripping away of all that had defined me – the power, the control, the illusion of superiority. It felt like my identity was being systematically eroded, the meticulously constructed self dissolving into a formless void.

Once carefully curated and manipulated, memories now flooded back unbidden, raw and unfiltered. Anya's face, once a pawn in my game, now appeared as a haunting reminder of my callous disregard for others' feelings. Sarah's terrified eyes reflected a guilt that consumed me, a guilt so profound and all-encompassing that it threatened to drown me in a sea of despair. The faces of my victims, each one a meticulously planned conquest, materialised in my mind's eye, their silent screams echoing in the desolate emptiness of my cell.

The hours stretched into an agonising eternity, punctuated only by the clang of metal on metal as the guards made their rounds. Each sound was a sharp reminder of my confinement, a physical manifestation of the loss of freedom. The carefully constructed order of my world, the meticulous routine that had once brought me a sense of perverse satisfaction, had been shattered. In its place was a chaotic disarray, a reflection of the turmoil raging within.

I attempted to recall the details of my elaborate plans, the intricate calculations, and the flawless execution. But the details were fuzzy, blurry, as if someone had deliberately smeared them with paint. My memory, usually so sharp and precise, was betraying me, another casualty in the devastating collapse of my carefully crafted reality. The details of my crimes, once so clear and carefully planned, seemed to elude me now, a deliberate self-defence mechanism, a desperate attempt to avoid the full weight of my guilt.

The cold, complex reality of my situation crashed like a tidal wave, washing away the vestiges of my self-deception. I was not a master manipulator, a puppet master pulling the strings of others' lives. I was a prisoner, trapped in a cage of my own making, a pathetic victim of my own self-destructive impulses.

My carefully constructed facade, the mask I had worn so skillfully, had been torn away, exposing the raw, vulnerable person beneath. This was not the performance I had planned, and there were no more scripts to follow, no more lines to memorise, no more audiences to impress. There was only the harsh, unrelenting reality of my actions and their devastating consequences. The carefully constructed narrative of my life, the illusion of control I had meticulously cultivated, had been irrevocably shattered. The unravelling was complete. The descent was over. And now, the long, dark night of reckoning hadbegun.

The harsh fluorescent lights of the examination room amplify the throbbing in my temples. Dr. Albright, a woman whose face held the weary wisdom of countless shattered minds, sat across from me, her expression impassive, a carefully constructed mask mirroring my past performances. The room is a sterile echo of my cell, a clinical white canvas devoid of the carefully chosen artefacts that had previously defined my spaces.

Here, there was no room for illusions.

She began with the basics, the standard battery of questions designed to assess cognitive function and emotional stability. Each question felt like a tiny probe, dissecting the carefully constructed layers of my psyche. Answered with the practised decision, I offered carefully curated responses designed to deflect her gaze and maintain a semblance of control. I described my sleep, or rather the lack thereof, as a fleeting distraction, a minor inconvenience. My appetite, I claimed, remained unaffected by my confinement. I spun tales of resilience, inner strength, and an unwavering resolve to confront the accusations levelled against me.

But beneath the surface, a tremor of unease was slowly escalating. The carefully constructed narrative, the script I had rehearsed countless times, felt increasingly brittle and strained. Dr. Albright's eyes, however, betrayed no surprise, no flicker of doubt. They were trained on me, dissecting my subtle tics, noting the almost imperceptible tremor in my hands and the brief hesitations before my responses. She was peeling back the layers, one carefully constructed sentence at a time.

She asked about my childhood, relationships, and the events that led to my current predicament. My carefully crafted answers, designed to present a picture of a rational, controlled individual, stumbled. The meticulously constructed facade crumbled under the weight of her probing questions. I evaded her gaze, my answers becoming fragmented and less precise. The meticulously rehearsed script faltered, revealing cracks in the foundation of my carefully built persona.

The silence that followed each response stretched, an uncomfortable void filled only by the rhythmic tick-tock of a clock on the wall – a relentless metronome marking the passage of time, the slow, inexorable erosion of my defences. The carefully constructed image of self-assured control I had meticulously maintained for so long was faltering, dissolving under the weight of her scrutiny.

My attempts to control the narrative and dictate the conversation's direction proved futile. Dr. Albright's questions were less direct interrogations and more subtle prompts, carefully designed to elicit deeper responses to pierce the carefully constructed layers of my defences. She delved into the intricacies of my past relationships, exploring the dynamics of power and control.

She asked about Anya, and her name lodged in my throat like a shard of glass. I tried to deflect the question, to brush it aside as a minor detail in the grand tapestry of my life. But the words caught in my throat, the carefully constructed narratives refusing to materialise. The image of Anya's face, previously a tool to be manipulated, now haunted me, a painful reminder of the devastating consequences of my actions.

She pressed me on Sarah, her name another painful reminder, a symbol of the irreversible damage I had inflicted. Once clear and sharply defined in my meticulously planned actions, the details now seemed indistinct, shrouded in a fog of self-preservation. My carefully constructed defences crumbled further, revealing a deep guilt and a chasm of self-loathing.

The clinical setting, once a stage for my performance, became a crucible, a space where my carefully crafted illusions were stripped bare, exposing the raw, vulnerable underbelly of my psyche. Dr. Albright's questions weren't accusations; they were surgical incisions, revealing the festering wounds beneath the surface. Each carefully measured question chipped away at my defences, exposing the fragility of my meticulouslyc onstructereality.

She delved into my meticulously planned crimes, her questions seemingly innocuous yet designed to uncover inconsistencies, to expose the cracks in my fabricated narratives.

Initially confident and assured, my responses became increasingly hesitant, punctuated by long pauses and evasive manoeuvres. The carefully orchestrated façade faltered. She noted my fidgeting, the subtle clenching of my jaw, and how my eyes darted nervously around the room. These were not mere observations; they were vital pieces of a complex puzzle, each tiny detail contributing to a larger picture, a comprehensive assessment of my mental state. The technical language she employed – "affective flattening," "limited emotional range," "signs of narcissistic personality disorder"

– felt like cold steel, each clinical term a precise description of my disintegration.

The session concluded with a provisional diagnosis. Histrionic personality disorder with antisocial features, she posited, a label that felt like a branding iron, etching a permanent mark on my soul. It was a diagnosis as clinical and precise as my meticulously planned crimes, a cold, hard judgment delivered with the same clinical detachment I had once wielded as a weapon. The careful construction of my life, elaborate schemes, and meticulously crafted illusions were alluded to by a clinical label. Leaving the examination room, the sterile white walls seemed to press in on me, amplifying the hollow ache in my chest. The carefully constructed world I had built, a world based on manipulation and control, had imploded. The weight of the diagnosis settled upon me, a tangible burden, a stark reminder of the damage I had inflicted, not only on others but also on myself. The therapeutic process, she had explained, was a long and arduous journey, a climb from the depths of a self-made abyss. His initial diagnosis was merely a marker, a point of departure, but the daunting path ahead seemed an overwhelming and crushing weight. The unravelling was far from over. It was only the beginning. The long, arduous task of rebuilding, if possible, lay ahead. Or was that simply another illusion? The question echoed in the sterile, white corridor, a haunting whisper in the silence. The clock ticked relentlessly on.

CHAPTER 3

THE CONFINES OF REALITY

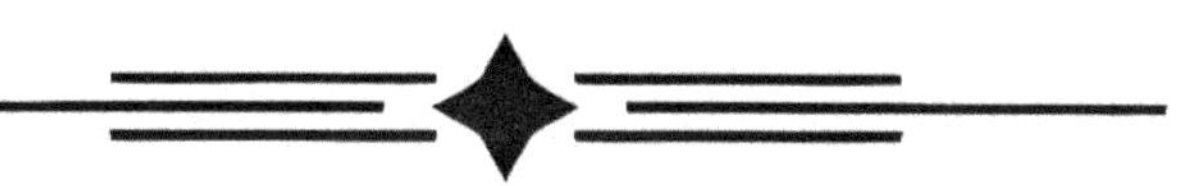

The steel door clanged shut behind me, the sound echoing the finality of my situation. The corridor stretched before me, a long, bleak tunnel of sterile white walls and echoing silence. The air hung heavy with the scent of disinfectant, a constant reminder of my confinement. This wasn't the carefully curated environment of my previous life; this was a place of stark reality, devoid of the comforting illusions I had so meticulously constructed. My cell was small, barely larger than a closet. A thin mattress lay on the floor, the springs digging into my back. A small metal table and chair were bolted to the floor, immutable fixtures in this unchanging landscape. The high, narrow window offered a limited view of a concrete courtyard, a bleak vista mirroring the desolation. There were no personal items, no photographs, no books – only the cold, complex reality of my incarceration.

The absence of any personal artefact felt like a stripping away of my identity, a deliberate effort to erase the carefully constructed persona I hadsopainstakinglcultivated.

The days bled into one another, a monotonous cycle of wakefulness and sleep punctuated by the rhythmic clang of doors and the distant shouts of other inmates. The routine was designed to strip away individuality, to reduce us to mere numbers, cogs in the vast machinery of the institution. Meals were served in silence, the bland, institutional food reflecting the emotional sterility of our surroundings. The lack of choice and enforced uniformity constantly reminded us of our powerlessness.

The silence was the most oppressive aspect of confinement. It wasn't a peaceful silence but a heavy, suffocating one, pregnant with unspoken anxieties and fears. It was a silence broken only by the occasional murmur of voices from down the hall, the rhythmic scrape of footsteps, or the distant, almost imperceptible sounds of distress from other inmates.

These fractured sounds served only to amplify the pervasive sense of isolation. It felt like the walls were closing in, pressing down on me, crushing the remnants of my carefully constructed self.

The daily interactions with the staff were perfunctory and devoid of warmth or empathy. They were figures of authority, faceless and emotionless, their actions governed by protocol and procedure. Their interactions were transactional, focused on the administration of medications, the monitoring of vital signs, and the maintenance of order. There was no attempt at understanding, no expression of compassion – only the cold, clinical detachment of those working to manage the broken. The lack of privacy was a constant source of anxiety. Every aspect of my existence was monitored, observed, and documented. My interactions with other inmates were brief and superficial, constrained by the ever-present surveillance. Even my most private thoughts felt exposed and vulnerable to scrutiny. The sense of being constantly watched and under constant observation fueled a pervasive sense of unease, a feeling that my carefully constructed façade was perpetually on the verge of collapse.

I spent hours staring at the wall, lost in my thoughts, replaying the events leading to my current predicament. The meticulous planning, the calculated risks, and the calculated manipulation seemed surreal, distant, almost like a dream.

The memory of Anya's face, once a carefully controlled tool in my repertoire, now haunted me, a constant reminder of the devastating consequences of my actions. Sarah's image, another painful reminder of the damage I had inflicted, served to chip away at the composure I had so diligently constructed.

Sleep offered little respite. The noises of the institution, the constant awareness of my confinement, and the nagging weight of guilt and self-loathing prevented me from achieving any semblance of restful sleep. My dreams were a chaotic jumble of fragmented memories, distorted faces, and relentless pursuers. Upon waking, I was left with a lingering feeling of anxiety, the crushing weight of reality pressing down on me.

The contrast between my former life and this brutal reality was stark. My previous life had been one of meticulous planning, calculated risks, and a carefully constructed persona that allowed me to manipulate and control others. I had built a world where I dictated the terms, where my desires reigned supreme. Now, I was stripped of all control, reduced to a passive observer of my unravelling. The world I had so carefully constructed had imploded, leaving me adrift in a sea of self-doubt and despair.

The institutional food was monotonous, tasteless, and

served in near silence. The repetitive nature of the meals mirrored the monotony of my existence. Each bite reminded me of my life's controlled, restricted nature, an experience vastly different from the carefully chosen, gourmet meals I once enjoyed. The blatant lack of culinary artistry was a painful contrast, fueling my resentment toward my present situation.

The sparse furniture in my cell was functional, devoid of any comfort or aesthetic appeal. The metal table and chair served their purpose but offered no comfort. Their simple utilitarian nature symbolised the institution's approach to its inhabitants: basic necessities, but nothing more. It highlighted the sharp contrast to my past, where every piece of furniture had been carefully selected to enhance my environment. It served as a tool to project an image of cultivated success and control.

The stark, white walls seemed to press in on me, amplifying the feeling of confinement and isolation. The absence of colour or decoration further reinforced the sterile and depressing nature of the environment. The lack of any personal items, any reminder of my previous

life, heightened my sense of loss and alienation. These

bare, unforgiving surfaces were a potent metaphor for stripping away my identity and dismantling my carefully constructed life.

Even the sound of the guards' footsteps echoed a sense of oppression, a constant reminder of the ever-present surveillance. Each clang of a metal door amplified the feeling of being trapped, a harsh reminder of my limitations. The seemingly random nature of these noises and the irregularity of their occurrence added a sense of unpredictability to my already bleak situation, causing a low-level anxiety to perpetually simmer.

The routine physical examinations were conducted with a clinical detachment that felt impersonal and dehumanising. The process lacked warmth or empathy, reducing me to a collection of measurable data points. The methodical examinations only emphasised my powerlessness and reinforced my sense of vulnerability. This was not healthcare; it was observation and control.

The enforced silence and lack of interaction with others left me struggling with a deep sense of isolation and loneliness. The absence of stimulating conversation or human connection was a deliberate strategy to control my environment. Still, this tactic only exacerbated the despair and hopelessness that had already begun to take hold. The silence was not a peaceful retreat but a cruel punishment, stripping me of any sense of belonging. The ever-present feeling of being watched, of having every action and reaction scrutinised, added to the suffocating sense of confinement. The institutional setting was designed to remove autonomy and control even the most minute details of my life. The loss of privacy and the constant awareness of being observed made it impossible to escape the oppressive weight of my situation, preventing any opportunity for privacy or escape.

Each passing day amplified the feeling of my own unravelling. The loss of control, the monotonous routine, and the crushing weight of guilt and self-loathing were slowly eroding my carefully constructed persona. The stark reality of my confinement had chipped away at the façade, revealing the vulnerability beneath. The process of disintegration was not an external imposition; it was a gradual, internal collapse. The institutional setting served as merely a catalyst.

The stark reality of my situation was becoming increasingly clear: my carefully constructed world was gone, reduced to nothing more than the sterile white walls surrounding me. The illusion of control, previously my shield, had shattered, leaving me exposed, vulnerable, and alone. The unravelling, I realised, was far from over. It was only just beginning.

The metallic tang of blood, faint but persistent, clung to the back of my throat. It wasn't a physical wound, not this time, but the taste of guilt, a bitter aftertaste to every thought, every memory that surfaced in the suffocating silence of my cell. Once merely oppressive, the walls seemed to pulse with the rhythm of my erratic heartbeat. The sterile white was no longer just a visual assault; it reflected my mind's stark, bleached landscape. The carefully constructed façade, the meticulously crafted persona, was crumbling, layer by layer, revealing the raw, bleeding core beneath.

It wasn't a sudden epiphany, this confrontation with reality. It wasn't a dramatic moment of clarity, a single, shattering revelation. It was a slow, agonising process, like watching a glacier calve, a piece at a time, until the whole structure finally yields to the relentless pressure of the truth. It began with small cracks in the meticulously built wall of denial – a fleeting image of Anya's terrified eyes, a whisper of Sarah's name in the dead of night, a phantom touch on my arm that sent shivers down my spine. Once carefully suppressed, these fragments began to coalesce, forming a mosaic of my past, a tapestry woven with threads of manipulation, deception, and, ultimately, profound damage.

The institutional routine, so meticulously designed to strip me of my identity, became a catalyst for self-reflection. The bland meals, the cold, hard surfaces, the relentless surveillance – these elements, once symbols of my powerlessness, now served as a backdrop against which I began to examine the true nature of my actions. Each repetitive task, each perfunctory interaction with the staff, chipped away at the carefully constructed barriers I had erected around my emotions. The silence, once a suffocating blanket, became a space for introspection, a crucible in which the   raw materials of my guilt and self-loathing were forged into a painful awareness.

The internal monologue became my constant companion, a relentless internal dialogue that echoed the anxieties and fears I had diligently suppressed. It was a torrent of accusations, a relentless barrage of self-recrimination.

I replayed every conversation and interaction, dissecting each word and gesture, searching for the precise moment when things had begun to unravel. I analysed my motivations, my manipulations, and my justifications. Was it ambition? A thirst for power? Or something far more insidious, rooted in a deep-seated pathology I had long ignored?

The answers, when they came, were agonisingly slow and painfully clear. My actions weren't the result of calculated strategy or cold-blooded ambition. They stemmed from a deep-seated, almost primal need for control, a need so powerful it eclipsed any sense of empathy, any consideration for the well-being of others. It was a desperate attempt to quell the chaos within, to impose order on a world that felt inherently unstable and threatening. The carefully constructed persona I had cultivated was not a mask but a desperate attempt to hide the fractured self beneath.

The vivid, sharp memory of Anya was no longer a tool, a pawn in my game of manipulation. It was a haunting reminder of the human cost of my actions, a constant source of profound remorse. Her fear, vulnerability, and utter helplessness—these emotions, once conveniently dismissed as collateral damage, now pierced my carefully constructed defences, exposing the depths of my cruelty. I could almost feel her pain, a visceral ache that echoed in my own shattered soul.

Sarah's image was equally devastating. Her innocence, her trust, the vulnerability she had placed in me – these were things I had ruthlessly exploited, shattering a life with calculated precision. The memory of her betrayed trust was a constant weight,acrushing burden that threatened to pull me under. It starkly contrasted the image I had projected to the world, the image of a successful, charming individual who had everything under control. The reality was starkly different – a portrait of a damaged individual incapable of genuine connection or empathy.

The trauma of my own childhood, long suppressed, began to surface in the form of fragmented memories and recurring nightmares. The abuse, the neglect, the constant fear – these were the roots of my pathology, the dark soil from which my destructive behaviours had grown.

The realisation was not an excuse but a painful acknowledgement of the forces that had shaped me, the wounds that had festered and ultimately poisoned my soul. Understanding my past didn't justify my actions, but it helped to contextualise them, to see the pattern of destruction that had woven itsthe way through my life.

The process of acceptance wasn't a linear one. There were moments of intense self-loathing, periods where the weight of my guilt threatened to consume me. There were nights when sleep offered no respite, when my dreams were haunted by the faces of those I had harmed, their accusing eyes piercing the darkness of my subconscious. There were moments when I desperately clung to the remnants of my old persona, a desperate attempt to reconstruct the carefully crafted illusion that had once protected me from the truth.

But the truth, relentless and unforgiving, kept chipping away at my defences. The sterile walls of my cell became a mirror, reflecting not just the physical confinement but the inner prison I had built for myself. The silence was no longer oppressive but a necessary space for introspection, a crucible where I could begin the agonising process of confronting the monster I had become. The monotonous routine was no longer a symbol of powerlessness but an opportunity for self-examination, a structured path through the labyrinth of my own guilt.

The realisation dawned slowly, painfully, that the only way out of this inner prison was through acceptance, acknowledging the extent of my actions and taking responsibility for the consequences. It was a daunting task, a Herculean effort to confront the dark recesses of my psyche, acknowledge the depth of my failings, and begin the long, arduous healing process. The journey would be long and arduous, fraught with setbacks and temptations to retreat into the comforting illusions of the past. But the first step, the crucial step, was to face the truth, to look into the abyss of my own soul and acknowledge the darkness within. The confines of reality, once a place of bleak despair, had become the starting point of my redemption. The journey was just beginning.

The fluorescent lights of Dr. Albright's office hummed, counterpoint to the frantic rhythm of my own heart. He sat across from me, his face an impassive mask, his eyes holding a depth that unnerved me. He didn't offer platitudes or attempt to soothe. He simply observed, a silent witness to the unravelling I was undergoing.

This was the third session since my incarceration, and the carefully constructed walls of my self-deception were crumbling under the weight of his incisive questions.

"Tell me about your childhood," he'd said, his voice a low murmur that cut through the silence like a surgeon's scalpel.

The words, initially reluctant, began to flow, a torrent of fragmented memories, long suppressed, rising to the surface like a toxic sludge. I spoke of the constant fear and the pervasive sense of insecurity that had permeated my early years. Of the cold, empty spaces within the imposing family home, spaces that mirrored the emotional void within myself. I spoke of the neglect, the subtle yet devastating acts of emotional abuse that had shaped my perception of the world, twisting it into a distortedreflectionofreality.

I described the chilling silence that often followed my father's outbursts, the silence that screamed louder than any shout. The silence taught me the crippling lesson that my feelings and needs were inconsequential and burdensome. The silence instilled within me a desperate need for control, a need to impose order upon a world that felt inherently chaotic and unpredictable.

Dr. Albright didn't interrupt, didn't offer reassurances. He listened, his gaze unwavering, allowing the narrative to unfold at its own pace. His silence, unlike the silence of my childhood, wasn't oppressive. It was a space, a canvas onto which I painted the bleak landscape of my past, a landscape I had long attempted to bury beneath layers of carefully crafted artifice.

The fragmented memories coalesced as I spoke, forming a more coherent picture. The picture was not pretty. It was a portrait of neglect, punctuated by moments of terrifying violence, the insidious poison of emotional abuse seeping into my very being. I remember the chilling feeling of isolation, the gnawing sense of worthlessness that had become an intrinsic part of my identity. I spoke of the manipulative games I played as a child, the desperate attempts to gain attention, to elicit even a flicker of warmth or connection. The sessions were agonising, each peeling back another layer of the protective shell I had built around myself. The tears came in waves, relentless, a physical manifestation of the pent-up emotions I had suppressed for so long. The shame was overwhelming, the weight of my past actions pressing down on me like a physical burden. But there was also a strange sense of liberation, a sense of release as I finally acknowledged the source of my pain, the root of my dysfunction.

Dr. Albright didn't judge. He didn't offer easy answers or empty platitudes. He challenged my justifications and questioned my narratives, guiding me towards a deeper understanding of my behaviour. He helped me to see the connection between my childhood trauma and the manipulative, destructive patterns that had characterised my adult life. He helped me to understand that my actions, though abhorrent, were not simply the product of cold-blooded calculation but the manifestation of a deep-seated pathology, a desperate attempt to control a world that had felt inherently uncontrollable.

We explored the concept of attachment and its crucial role in shaping my personality. He helped me understand the impact of the lack of secure attachment in my childhood and the way it had left me with a profound sense of insecurity, a deep-seated fear of abandonment. This fear, he explained, had driven my compulsive need for control, my relentless pursuit of power. The manipulation and the deceit were not merely conscious choices but desperate attempts to create an illusion of stability and fill the void left by a childhood starved of genuine connection.

The sessions were exhausting, both emotionally and mentally. I left each session drained and emotionally raw yet strangely invigorated. The process was akin to undergoing a major surgery: painful and invasive yet ultimately necessary for healing. I revisited memories that had haunted my dreams for years, memories I had carefully suppressed, locked away in the deepest recesses of my mind. We dissected my relationship with Anya and Sarah, exploring the power and control dynamics underpinning those interactions. Dr. Albright helped me see the extent of the damage I had caused, not just to the victims but also to myself. He helped me confront the monster I had become to acknowledge the darkness within. But he also helped me see the possibility of redemption, the healing potential. He didn't offer false hope; he simply provided a path, a way forward, through the tangled maze of my guilt and self-loathing.

The process of confronting my past was not a linear one. There were moments of intense regression, times when the weight of my actions threatened to overwhelm me, to pull me back into the darkness. There were sessions where I retreated behind the carefully constructed facade of my old persona, clinging to the comforting illusions of the past. But each time, Dr. Albright gently, persistently guided me back, helping me to confront the painful truth, to acknowledge the extent of my failures, and to take responsibility for my actions. He helped me understand that my past didn't justify my actions but provided a crucial context, a framework for understanding the origins of my destructive behaviour. He helped me to see that my pathology wasn't a death sentence but a condition that could be addressed, a wound that could be healed, albeit slowly, painfully, and with tremendous effort. The journey was far from over. The path ahead remained long and arduous, fraught with challenges and setbacks. But for the first

time, I felt a glimmer of hope, a faint light in the suffocating darkness. The confines of reality, once a prison, were slowly transforming into a space for healing, growth, and the arduous, painstaking work of redemption. The taste of blood, that metallic tang in my mouth, began to subside, replaced by a subtle taste of something else – a faint, almost imperceptible, hint of hope.

The image flickered – a shard of memory, sharp and brutal. A small hand, mine, clutching a porcelain doll, its painted eyes staring blankly ahead. The doll was a stark contrast to the chaos swirling around me. The air was thick with the stench of stale cigarette smoke and something else, something acrid, something akin to fear. My father's booming voice, a Thunderclap that shattered the fragile peace of the evening. The sharp crack of wood against the flesh, the choked sob that followed, swallowed by the suffocating silence that always descended afterwards. The silence was a heavy blanket, stifling, suffocating, a tangible entity that pressed down on me, crushing the breath from my lungs. I remember the chilling cold of the floor against my cheek, the dampness seeping into my skin, the taste of dust and fear on my tongue.

These fragments, these splinters of memory, pierced through the carefully constructed façade I had built around myself, revealing the raw, unfiltered horror of my childhood. They weren't cohesive narratives; they were glimpses, fleeting images, impressions that clung to the edges of my consciousness, surfacing unexpectedly, unbidden. These fragments coalesced in Dr. Albright's office, forming a disturbingly clear picture of my past. It was a picture painted in shades of grey, punctuated by splashes of stark, brutal black.

The neglect wasn't overt; it was a slow, insidious poison that seeped into every aspect of my life. It was in the averted gazes, the unanswered questions, and the cold, uncaring silence that echoed through the cavernous halls of our family home. It was in the unspoken expectations, the crushing weight of unspoken needs that were never met or acknowledged. It was the feeling of being invisible, unheard, a ghost inhabiting a life devoid of warmth, connection, or genuine love.

I remember the endless hours spent alone, the oppressive loneliness that clung to me like a second skin. I remember the games I played to fill the void, the desperate attempts to create a world where I could control the chaos and dictate the rules. I built elaborate castles from blankets and pillows, creating fantastical realms in which I reigned supreme. These games, these elaborate fantasies, were not simply childish diversions; they were desperate attempts to escape the reality of my life, to construct a world where I felt safe, loved, and valued.

The violence, when it came, was sporadic and unpredictable. It wasn't the constant, unrelenting brutality of some children's experiences; it was the intermittent bursts of rage, the terrifying outbursts that left me trembling in their wake. These weren't just physical blows; they were verbal assaults, a relentless barrage of criticism and contempt. The words, sharp and cruel, carved deep wounds into my psyche, leaving scars that would never fully heal. The words echoed in my head, a constant, insidious soundtrack to my existence.

They were the words that told me I was worthless, unlovable, a burden.

But the silence, the oppressive, suffocating silence that followed the outbursts, was arguably even worse. It was the silence of neglect, the deafening silence of indifference. It was the silence that screamed louder than any shout, the silence that taught me that my feelings, my needs, were inconsequential, burdensome, and unwanted. This silence instilled in me a desperate, almost pathological need for control, a need to impose order on a world that felt inherently chaotic and unpredictable. The need for control became my shield, my weapon, and my only defence against the terrifying instability of my early life.

As I spoke to Dr. Albright, the memories came flooding back, a relentless torrent of images and emotions. There were the dreams, the recurring nightmares that plagued my sleep, vivid and horrifying visions of shadows and darkness, echoing the fear that haunted my waking hours. These dreams weren't just symbolic representations of my trauma; they were visceral re-enactments, replays of the events that had shaped my life, twisting and distorting them into monstrous parodies of reality.

In these dreams, the silence was a malevolent entity, a living darkness that pursued me through shadowy corridors and labyrinthine spaces. The shadows seemed to writhe and twist, forming monstrous shapes that lunged at me from the darkness. The feeling of helplessness was overwhelming, the terror palpable, a crushing weight that pressed down on my chest, stealing my breath. I woke up screaming, drenched in sweat, the residue of fear clinging to my skin.

Dr. Albright helped me to interpret these dreams, to see them not merely as random collections of images but as symbolic representations of my suppressed trauma. He helped me to see the connections between the dreams, the fragmented memories, and the destructive patterns that characterised my adult life. He explained how my subconscious was attempting to process the trauma, to make sense of the chaos and disorder that had defined my early years.

The process was agonising, each session peeling away another layer of the protective shell I had constructed around myself. The tears came easily, relentless, a physical manifestation of the suppressed emotions I had carried for so long. The shame was overwhelming, the weight of my actions pressing down on me, a physical burden that threatened to crush me. But amidst the pain, there was a glimmer of something else, a strange sense of liberation, of release, as I finally acknowledged the source of my pain, the root of my dysfunction.

The understanding, however, did not bring immediate peace. It was a complex, torturous excavation of the self, a journey into my mind's deepest, darkest recesses. There were days when the memories hit with the force of a physical blow, leaving me gasping for breath, my body wracked with tremors. There were days when I felt utterly lost, overwhelmed by the enormity of my past, questioning the very foundation of my identity. There were moments when the urge to retreat, to slip back into the comforting illusion of denial, was almost irresistible.

Yet, the sessions were more than a mere cathartic release. Dr. Albright's approach wasn't simply about acknowledging the trauma; it was about understanding its impact and its insidious influence on my thoughts, feelings, and actions. He helped me to see how my childhood experiences had shaped my worldview, twisting it into a distorted, fragmented reflection of reality. He helped me to understand how my need for control stemmed from a profound sense of insecurity, a desperate attempt to impose order on a world that had always felt chaotic and unpredictable.

He explored the concept of attachment with me, highlighting the absence of secure

attachment in my formative years and its profound impact on my ability to form healthy relationships. He explained how the lack of a secure base and the absence of consistent love and support had left me with a deep-seated fear of abandonment. This fear drove my manipulative behaviours and my relentless pursuit of power and control. The manipulation and the deceit weren't simply conscious choices; they were desperate attempts to create an illusion of stability, to fill the void left by a childhood starved of genuine connection.

Through this painstaking process of self-discovery, I began to understand the intricate, deeply intertwined relationship between my past trauma and my present behaviour.
Though abhorrent, I began to see that my actions were not simply the product of cold-blooded calculation; they were the manifestations of a deep-seated pathology, a desperate attempt to control a world that had always felt uncontrollable.

The journey was far from over, the path ahead long and arduous. But for the first time, I saw a possibility, a faint glimmer of hope in the suffocating darkness that had enshrouded me for so long. The confines of reality, once a prison, were slowly transforming into a space for healing, growth, and the arduous, painstaking work of redemption.

The revelation of my past didn't bring a sense of catharsis; it brought a crushing weight, a physical manifestation of guilt that pressed down on my chest, making each breath a laboured struggle. It wasn't a simple feeling of remorse; it was a monstrous entity, a sentient darkness that coiled around my heart, squeezing the life out of me. It was the weight of a thousand lives, the shattered remnants of relationships, and the pain I had inflicted on those I claimed to love. The faces of my victims – their expressions of betrayal, fear, and devastation – haunted my waking hours and invaded the sanctuary of my sleep. They were no longer shadowy figures in the periphery of my dreams but tangible presences, their eyes burning into my soul, accusing, judging.

Their pain was my pain, amplified, magnified, twisted into a grotesque reflection of my offering. I had hurt them profoundly, irrevocably. And in hurting them, I had hurt myself, tearing apart the fragile threads of my sanity. The self-loathing was a relentless tide, pulling me under and drowning me in a sea of despair. It wasn't just the memory of my actions; it was the understanding of the motivations behind them – the desperate need for control, born from a childhood steeped in neglect and violence. From relieving the burden, amp that knowledge lifted it, making it even more unbearable.

Each night, I replayed the events in my mind, dissecting them, analysing them, and trying to find some semblance of justification and mitigating circumstance. But there was none. Your actions were deliberate, calculated, and driven by a selfish need for power and control. There was no accidental cruelty or impulsive recklessness, only cold, calculated manipulation. The chilling realisation that this was not a momentary lapse in judgment but a deeply ingrained pattern of behaviour was the most horrifying revelation.

The faces of their families, their expressions of grief, rage, and despair, were etched into

my mind. The accusations, the condemnation, the burning hatred in their eyes—it was a torment that surpassed any physical pain. I saw myself reflected in their eyes, not as a person, but as an embodiment of evil, a destroyer of lives. I saw the irreparable damage I had caused, the wounds that could never fully heal. Dr. Albright helped me navigate this treacherous terrain with his calm demeanour and unwavering empathy. He acknowledged the enormity of my guilt, validating its intensity without condoning my actions. He explained that guilt, in its raw, unfiltered form, wasn't a sign of weakness; it was a testament to my capacity for empathy, a recognition of the harm I had caused. He helped me understand that acknowledging my guilt wasn't an admission of defeat; it was the first step towards healing, towards making amends as much as possible.

He introduced me to the concept of restorative justice, emphasising my responsibility to accept the consequences of my actions and the possibility of engaging in acts of reparation, though not necessarily to the same extent that would undo what had been done. This wasn't absolution; it was about accountability, facing the truth and attempting to make things right, to some measure, however small. The concept was overwhelming, almost impossible to grasp, but the seed of hope that it planted within me offered a glimmer of light in the profound darkness.

But the path to acceptance wasn't linear; it was a tortuous journey through a landscape of despair and self-loathing. There were days when the weight of my guilt felt too heavy to bear, days when the urge to succumb to the darkness, to give in to the overwhelming tide of self-destruction, was almost irresistible. I battled with suicidal thoughts, the ultimate escape from the unbearable weight of my actions.

These thoughts were not a cry for attention; they were an authentic reflection of my profound inner torment. I wanted to erase myself from existence, to undo the damage, to alleviate, in the only way I could fathom, the pain I had caused.

The nightmares returned, more vivid and more terrifying than before. They weren't just plays of my past actions but horrifying visions of the suffering I had inflicted, magnified, grotesquely distorted. The faces of my victims morphed into monstrous figures, their cries of anguish echoing through the desolate landscapes of my dreams. Would wake up screaming, drenched in sweat, my heart pounding, the residue of terror clinging to me like a second skin.

Dr. Albright helped me understand that these dreams were a manifestation of my unconscious mind's attempts to process the trauma, to confront the unacknowledged pain and guilt that had been festering within me. He guided me through techniques of cognitive processing therapy, helping me to reframe my negative thoughts and challenge the self-destructive narratives that dominated my internal dialogue. Slowly, painstakingly, I began to dismantle the walls I had constructed around my guilt, allowing myself to experience the full spectrum of my emotions, even the unbearable ones.

However small, there were moments of progress that offered glimpses of hope. These were

the moments when I could acknowledge my actions without collapsing under the weight of self-reproach, begin to accept responsibility without succumbing to self-annihilation and achieve milestones and hard victories in a war against myself. The process was agonisingly slow and often felt hopeless, but I persevered, driven by the faint, fragile spark of a desire for redemption.

The healing process was not just about confronting my past; it was about rebuilding my life and creating a future where I could live with the consequences of my actions while attempting to make amends and find a path towards a meaningful existence. It was about learning to live with the unbearable weight of guilt, acknowledging it, owning it, and using it as fuel to drive towards a life dedicated to atonement and healing. This journey was far from over, the path long and arduous. Still, the faint light of hope, flickering in the suffocating darkness of my soul, was a testament to the enduring power of the human spirit to confront even the most profound darkness and emerge, however scarred, into the light. The weight of guilt remained a heavy burden that would likely always be a part of me. Still, now, it was a burden I was learning to carry with the strength and determination forged in the fires of self-reflection, remorse, and the relentless pursuit of redemption.

CHAPTER 4

FRAGMENTS OF MEMORY

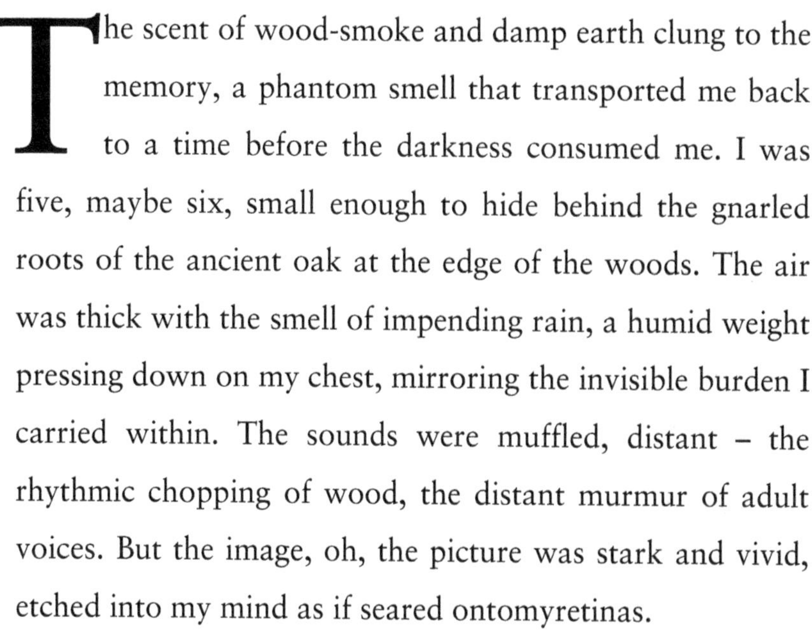

The scent of wood-smoke and damp earth clung to the memory, a phantom smell that transported me back to a time before the darkness consumed me. I was five, maybe six, small enough to hide behind the gnarled roots of the ancient oak at the edge of the woods. The air was thick with the smell of impending rain, a humid weight pressing down on my chest, mirroring the invisible burden I carried within. The sounds were muffled, distant – the rhythmic chopping of wood, the distant murmur of adult voices. But the image, oh, the picture was stark and vivid, etched into my mind as if seared ontomyretinas.

My father, his face shadowed and contorted, his hands moving with terrifying precision, wielded an axe. Not a woodsman's axe, careful and measured in its strokes, but an instrument of violence, wielded with a savage, unrestrained fury. The target wasn't a tree, but my mother, her back turned, her body a fragile thing against the brutal force of his rage. I remember the splintering of wood, not of a tree trunk, but of something far more delicate and precious. A chair, I think, shattered into a thousand pieces. The scream, however, was unmistakable, a raw, primal sound that tore through the stillness of the woods, a sound that still echoes in the desolate chambers of my mind. Then, silence. A heavy, suffocating silence punctuated only by the rhythmic rain drip from the oak leaves. I didn't move, didn't breathe. My small body was rigid, paralysed by a terror that went beyond understanding. It was a visceral knowledge, a primal sense of violence, a chilling premonition of the darkness that would consume my life. The rain began to fall, washing away the blood and the sound, not the image.

Not the memory. That remained, a gruesome tableau painted in the deepest shades of fear and despair.

Later, I was found, shivering and soaked, huddled beneath the protective embrace of the ancient oak. My mother, her face pale and drawn, her eyes hollowed by an unimaginable sorrow, held me close. But her embrace didn't offer solace. It was a fragile shield against a storm that raged within her, a storm that I, in my innocent childhood, could not comprehend. There was a coldness in her eyes, a detachment that chilled me to the bone, a silent acknowledgement of a world devoid of love and protection. Her silence spoke volumes, a chilling testament to the unspoken pain that permeated our lives.

Other fragments, like shards of broken glass, pierced the veil of my repressed memories.

The smell of stale cigarettes and cheap whiskey, a suffocating aroma that clung to the air in our small, cramped apartment. The rasping cough that shook my father's body, a sound that resonated with the unspoken violence that permeated our lives. His hand, heavy and brutal, struck out at random, leaving bruises and welts that mirrored the invisible wounds that festered in my soul. My mother's pleading, hushed whispers were swallowed by the ever-present silence. The fear etched upon her face, her eyes mirroring the terror that was my constant companion.

I remember the heavy, oppressive silence that was as much a part of our lives as the air we breathed. It was a silence filled with unspoken words, unresolved conflicts, and a suppressed rage that simmered beneath the surface of our dysfunctional family. It nurtured the seeds of darkness, allowing the violence to fester and grow, feeding upon the unspoken pain that bound ustogether.

There was a recurring image – a flickering candlelight illuminating a shadowed corner of the room. My mother, hunched over, rocking back and forth, whispering unintelligible words, her face etched with an unimaginable grief. I didn't understand then, but I know now. It was the silent scream of a woman trapped in a world of abuse, her spirit broken, her will to fight eroded by years of relentless violence. Her eyes, wide and haunted, bore witness to a suffering that surpassed any physical pain.

The memories were not chronological; they were disjointed and fragmented, like pieces of a shattered mirror reflecting a distorted image of my past. They were glimpses, fleeting moments of terror, fear, and despair. But they were real. They were the building blocks of the fractured person I had become, the seeds of the darkness that had grown within me, twisting my soul into a grotesque parody of its former self.

One memory stands out with brutal clarity: a sharp, searing pain, a burning sensation that seared itself into my memory. The taste of blood, metallic and acrid, filled my mouth. The sight of my own hand, small and bleeding, trembling uncontrollably. I remember the confusion, the bewilderment, the inability to understand why I had been hurt, why I was deserving of such violence. But the memory is devoid of context, a single, isolated incident, a jarring moment of trauma that was somehow interwoven with the tapestry of my childhood.

The psychological impact was devastating. The pervasive fear, the constant feeling of being on edge, the inability to trust, and the overwhelming sense of helplessness – these were the hallmarks of my childhood. I learned to anticipate violence, to readthe subtle cues that signalled my father's impending rage, and to become adept at avoiding his unpredictable outbursts. I developed hyper-vigilance, an acute awareness of my surroundings, a constant scanning for potential threats. This became my survival mechanism, a defence against a world where violence was an ever-present threat.

My childhood was a battleground, a landscape of fear and uncertainty. There was no safe space, no refuge from the violence that permeated our lives. I learned to suppress my emotions, to bury my feelings deep within, to mask the pain that gnawed at my soul. This repression, this constant suppression of my feelings, became a prison, a cage built from fear and silence. It was a prison I had inhabited for years, from which it seemed impossible to escape.

The fragmented memories were more than just recollections of events; they were fragments of a shattered self, the pieces of a life that had been ripped apart by violence and neglect. They were the keys to understanding the origins of the darkness that had taken root within me, the darkness that I had spent so many years struggling to control, contain, and keep from overwhelming me. These memories were the genesis of my actions, the roots of the guilt that haunted me, the foundation of the person I had become. Confronting them, understanding them, was the first step towards healing, towards dismantling the destructive patterns that had shaped my life. The path was long and arduous, filled with pain and self-doubt, but it was a path I had to tread, a journey I had to undertake if I were ever to find peace. The road to redemption would never be easy, but there was a profound need to walk the path.

The rain continued relentlessly drumming against the windowpane, mirroring the relentless pounding in my head.

The fragmented memories, once elusive whispers, now clawed their way to the surface, a relentless tide of horror threatening to drown me. It wasn't just the physical violence; it was the insidious erosion of my sense of self, the slow, deliberate dismantling of my inner world. My father's rage was a blunt instrument, shattering the fragile structure of my childhood, but it was the chilling indifference of my mother that truly carved the deepest wounds.

Her silence was a deafening roar, a constant, suffocating presence that choked the life out of my spirit. She wasn't actively participating in the violence, yet her passive acceptance, her inability or unwillingness to intervene, created a vacuum where hope and security should have thrived. It was a chilling form of complicity, a silent endorsement of the violence that consumed our lives. She became a ghost, a pale, spectral figure haunting the periphery of my existence, her eyes mirroring despair so profound it seemed to suck the very air from the room. I learned early on that tears, pleas, cries for help – none of it mattered. The silence swallowed them all, leaving only a gnawing emptiness and a chilling certainty: I was alone.

The genetic predisposition, the inherited vulnerability – I began to see how these factors intertwined with my environment to create the perfect storm. My research into the neurobiology of violence and the complex interplay of genetics and environment began to illuminate the darkness within me. It wasn't just nurture, wasn't just the brutal reality of my childhood; it was a confluence of factors, a perfect alignment of biological vulnerability and environmental triggers that forged the predator I became.

The studies on the amygdala, the brain region responsible for processing fear and aggression, came to mind. The countless studies demonstrating the impact of early childhood trauma on brain development, the altered neural pathways, the heightened reactivity to threats – all of it began to fit together, forming a chillingly coherent picture of my own transformation. The hyper-vigilance, the acute awareness of my surroundings, the constant scanning for potential threats – these weren't just survival mechanisms; they were manifestations of a damaged brain, rewired by trauma and shaped by the relentless pressure of fear.

The lack of nurturing and a secure attachment figure had devastating consequences. Attachment theory, Bowlby's groundbreaking work, suddenly became terrifyingly relevant. The failure to develop healthy attachments in early childhood and the absence of a safe haven where I could explore the world without fear left me adrift in a sea of uncertainty and insecurity. This lack of secure attachment profoundly impacted my ability to form healthy relationships, trust others, and experience empathy.

My own actions, the violence I inflicted, were not random, not simply the result of some innate evil. They were the product of a deeply disturbed mind, a mind shaped by trauma, by neglect, by the absence of love and understanding. They were the distorted expression of my inner turmoil, the desperate attempt to control the chaos that had consumed my life. The thrill, the power, the perverse sense of control I derived from my actions – these were compensatory mechanisms, desperate attempts to fill the void left by years of emotional deprivation. It was a cruel irony, a twisted parody of normalcy, a desperate attempt to find meaning in a world that had offered me only pain and suffering.

I began to dissect the seemingly random acts of violence, the impulsive outbursts of rage that had marked my life. They weren't random at all; they were meticulously crafted expressions of deeply rooted trauma, carefully orchestrated to maintain a semblance of control in a world that felt utterly chaotic. Each act of violence was a desperate attempt to assert control, to fill the void left by the powerlessness I felt as a child. It was a futile attempt to silence the inner turmoil, the relentless barrage of negative emotions that had haunted me for years.

The self-destructive tendencies, the cycles of self-harm and reckless behaviour were also manifestations of this underlying trauma. They were desperate cries for help disguised as self-inflicted wounds, a twisted form of communication that screamed out into the void. The cutting, the burning, and the risk-taking behaviours were attempts to regain control, to exert some influence over a life that had felt entirely out of my hands.

But there was another layer, a darker, more insidious element. The pleasure, the perverse satisfaction I derived from inflicting pain – it wasn't simply sadism, not a simple thirst for violence. It was a twisted form of retribution, a desperate attempt to impose the pain I had suffered on others. It was a way of levelling the playing field, of finding a perverse sense of balance in a world that had felt profoundly unjust. It was a grotesque attempt to regain control, to assert my dominance in a world where I had been so utterly powerless. As I delved deeper into the dark recesses of my mind, I realised that the trauma hadn't just created a monster; it had instilled in me a chilling sense of justification for my actions.

The memories continued to flood back, each one a fresh wound, a painful reminder of the brutal reality of my childhood. I recalled a specific incident, a chillingly vivid memory of a younger me, perhaps seven or eight years old, huddled beneath the kitchen table, listening to my parents' arguments. Their voices, laced with venom, echoed through the cramped apartment, the words blurred and indistinct, yet the raw emotion palpable. My father's rage, his threats, the fear in my mother's voice – it was a symphony of terror, a nightmarish soundtrack to my childhood. I remember crawling further under the table, desperate to disappear, to become invisible, to escape the torrent of hatred and violence that surrounded me.

This incident, and countless others like it, left indelible marks on my psyche. The constant fear, hyper-vigilance, and inability to trust became ingrained in my personality. I learned to anticipate violence, to read the subtle cues that signalled my father's impending rage, and to become adept at avoiding his unpredictable outbursts. But the constant state of fear also warped my perception of reality, twisting my understanding of relationships, love, and trust.

The world I inhabited was a distorted reflection of reality, a warped landscape where violence was the norm, where safety was an illusion, and where love was a foreign concept. The absence of a stable, loving environment had created a void in my soul, a void that I desperately tried to fill with perverse acts of control and dominance. The cycle of abuse, the insidious erosion of my sense of self, the constant fear and anxiety – these were not merely the circumstances of my childhood; they were the building blocks of my monstrous transformation.

The creation of a monster is not a sudden, dramatic event. It's a slow, insidious process, a gradual erosion of the self, a twisted metamorphosis fueled by trauma, neglect, and the absence of love. It's a process that begins in childhood, shaping the very fabric of one's being. The interplay of genetic predisposition and environmental factors, the impact of early childhood trauma on brain development, and the failure to develop healthy attachments – these are not merely academic concepts; they are the keys to understanding the origins of violence, the roots of the darkness that consumes some of us. The fragmented memories were more than just recollections of events; they were the building blocks of a fractured self, the raw materials from which the monster was forged. They were the evidence, the irrefutable proof of the creation of a monster.

But they were also the pathway to understanding, the first step towards healing. Confronting these memories and accepting the brutal truth of my past was the only way to begin to dismantle the destructive patterns that had shaped my life. The road to redemption was long and arduous, filled with pain and self-doubt, but it was a journey I was determined to undertake. Even a monster can yearn for redemption, a chance to escape the darkness that had consumed them. The journey would be long and arduous, but the hope of redemption, however faint, was a flicker of light in the suffocating darkness.

The rain lashed against the windows, a relentless rhythm mirroring my mind's chaotic pulse. The memories, sharp shards of glass in the swirling vortex of my consciousness,..continued to surface. But now, a new layer of understanding began to coalesce, a chilling recognition of the elaborate façade I had constructed—the illusion of control.

It wasn't simply a matter of justifying my actions; it was a far more insidious process, a meticulously crafted performance played out on the stage of my own mind. Each act of violence and transgression was meticulously planned, not in the meticulous detail of a strategic military operation, but in the carefully choreographed movements of a disturbed mind seeking to orchestrate a narrative of dominance. I was the director, the actor, and the audience all rolled into one. I controlled the script, even if the script was born from the deepest recesses of my tormentedpsyche.

This delusion of control was a twisted coping mechanism, a desperate attempt to impose order on the chaotic landscape of my inner world. The unpredictable outbursts of rage, the seemingly random acts of violence—these were not random at all. They were carefully orchestrated acts designed to create a sense of power and agency in a world that had consistently robbed me of both. Each victim was a pawn in my macabre game, a silent participant in the drama I had meticulously created.

The cognitive dissonance was staggering. I knew, intellectually, that my actions were horrific, that they inflicted unimaginable pain and suffering on others. Yet, within the confines of my distorted reality, I perceived myself as a puppeteer, pulling the strings of fate and directing the narrative according to my twisted desires. This was not a simple denial of responsibility; it was a profound and pervasive delusion, a meticulously constructed worldview that allowed me to compartmentalise my guilt, to separate the monstrous acts from the flawed, yet somehow still fundamentally me, who performed them.

The pleasure derived from my actions wasn't simply the thrill of the hunt; it was the perverse satisfaction of controlling the narrative, of orchestrating the downfall of others. It was the ultimate affirmation of my warped sense of self-worth. The meticulous planning, the anticipation of the act, and the careful execution were not the hallmarks of a mindless brute, but the calculations of a mind perversely focused on control.

I remember one specific incident, the abduction and subsequent... disposal... of a young woman. In my memory, it's not a chaotic scramble, a brutal and unplanned assault. Instead, it's a meticulously staged event. I recall the careful selection of the location, the meticulous planning of the route, and the precise timing of every movement. Even the disposal itself, the cold, calculated act of eliminating all traces of my presence, was an exercise in precision and control. I think it wasn't a horrific crime but a theatrical performance crafted with meticulous attention to detail.

The illusion of control extended beyond the immediate act of violence itself. It permeated every aspect of my life, from the carefully constructed façade I presented to the outside world to the meticulously planned routines that governed my daily existence. I was a master of deception, a skilled illusionist, weaving a web of lies and subterfuge to maintain the illusion of normalcy while secretly orchestrating my macabre dramas in the shadows.

This delusion of control was deeply rooted in my childhood trauma. The powerlessness I experienced as a child, the constant fear and anxiety, and the utter lack of control over my own life—these experiences left an indelible mark on my psyche. The acts of violence were not just a release of pent-up rage; they were a desperate attempt to reclaim the control that had been so brutally stolen from me.

The illusion of control allowed me to compartmentalise my guilt, to separate the horrifying reality of my actions from the carefully constructed narrative I had created in my mind. This compartmentalisation was a critical component of my survival mechanism. It allowed me to function and maintain a semblance of normalcy while simultaneously indulging in my dark impulses. It was a form of self-deception so profound, so deeply ingrained, that it became indistinguishable from reality.

The cognitive dissonance between my intellectual understanding of the horror of my actions and my delusional belief in my control over them created a constant internal conflict. It was a war waged within the confines of my own mind, a battle between the monstrous impulses that drove me and the vestiges of my former self, the remnants of a conscience that had not been entirely extinguished. This inner turmoil manifested itself in various ways, from fleeting moments of doubt and self-recrimination to periods of intense anxiety and paranoia.

The paranoia was particularly acute following each act of violence. The fear of being caught, of having my carefully constructed façade shattered, gnawed at my sanity. I would become hyper-vigilant, constantly scanning my surroundings for signs of danger, convinced that the authorities were closing in and that my meticulously crafted illusion was about to crumble. This fear wasn't a rational response to the inherent risks associated with my actions; it was a manifestation of my deep-seated insecurity, a desperate attempt to maintain control in the face of an ever-present threat to my carefully constructed reality. The cognitive distortions were profound and pervasive. I minimised the suffering of my victims, rationalising my actions as necessary evils, acts of retribution or punishment for their perceived transgressions. I magnified my own importance, believing that my actions were justified and that I was playing a crucial role in a grand, albeit twisted, narrative. I projected my own feelings of inadequacy and self-hatred onto my victims, justifying my acts of violence as a necessary means of eliminating the perceived threats they represented.

The illusion of control was a shield, a carefully constructed barrier that protected me from the overwhelming guilt and self-loathing that would have otherwise consumed me. But it was also a prison, a self-imposed confinement that prevented me from honestly confronting the darkness within and from acknowledging the full extent of my depravity. The illusion, however potent, was ultimately fragile, a thin veneer masking the chaotic depths of my psyche. As the fragmented memories continued to surface, the cracks in this meticulously constructed façade widened, threatening to expose the monstrous truth beneath. The rain outside continued its relentless drumming, a soundtrack to my carefully constructed reality's slow, agonising unravelling. The illusion began shattering, and the terrifying truth was slowly emerging.

The flickering fluorescent light of my office cast long shadows across the worn, leather armchair. He sat rigidly, his hands clasped tightly in his lap, starkly contrasting the tempestuous narrative he'd unleashed in the previous sessions. The man before me, let's call him Patient X, presented a chilling paradox: a meticulously constructed façade of normalcy masking a profound and terrifying abyss of violence and delusion. His confession, delivered in measured tones that belied the horrific nature of his crimes, was a testament to his exceptional ability to compartmentalise, a skill honed over years of carefully cultivated self-deception.

My role, as his therapist, was not merely to understand his actions but to navigate the treacherous terrain of his mind, to unravel the intricate web of cognitive distortions and delusions that sustained his terrifying charade. It was a daunting task that demanded a delicate balance of empathy and professional detachment. One misstep, a misplaced word, a misjudged gesture, could send him spiralling into a defensive retreat, further solidifying the walls of his self-constructed prison.

The diagnostic picture was complex. While elements of antisocial personality disorder were evident—the lack of remorse, the callous disregard for the suffering of others, the manipulative behaviour—it was far more nuanced than a simple label. The meticulous planning, the theatrical nature of his crimes, the profound delusion of control—these suggested a deeper pathology, a more intricate and sinister dance between conscious awareness and deeply ingrained, unconscious drives. I suspected a significant narcissistic component, fuelling his need for control and his perverse sense of grandiosity. The meticulously crafted narratives surrounding his acts of violence weren't simply justifications; they were integral to his self-image, a twisted self-mythology that allowed him to maintain a fragile sense of self-worth.

The absence of genuine empathy was striking. He described his victims with a clinical detachment, focusing on the logistical details of his crimes rather than the human suffering they entailed. His voice had no emotional resonance, no flicker of remorse in his eyes. This lack of empathy wasn't simply a symptom of his disorder; it was a critical component of his survival mechanism, a necessary shield against the overwhelming guilt and self-loathing that his actions should have evoked.

But the absence of empathy didn't translate to a complete absence of emotion. Beneath the surface were hints of something else—a simmering rage, a deep-seated insecurity, a profound sense of powerlessness that seemed to fuel his need for control. This underlying emotional turmoil manifested in various ways, from subtle shifts in his demeanour to outbursts of irritability and frustration. The meticulous planning of his actions and the careful construction of his alibis were not solely driven by a..desire to evade capture; they were also an attempt to manage his internal chaos and impose order on his psyche's turbulent landscape.

The challenge lay in penetrating this meticulously constructed façade, in gaining access to the raw emotions simmering beneath the surface. Traditional therapeutic approaches proved inadequate. He was a master manipulator, adept at deflecting questions, twisting interpretations, and constructing narratives that served his self-serving purposes. I needed a different strategy, a more nuanced approach that would allow me to circumvent his defences and gain access to the core of his pathology.

My approach involved a carefully calibrated blend of confrontation and empathy. I challenged his narratives gently but firmly, forcing him to confront the inconsistencies in his stories and the gaps in his logic. But I also showed empathy, acknowledging the trauma he had endured in his childhood and validating his feelings of powerlessness and anger while never condoning his actions. The goal was not to make him feel judged or shamed but to create a safe space where he could begin to explore the painful emotions that drove his behaviour.

The process was slow, painstaking, and often frustrating. There were setbacks, intense resistance, and periods when he retreated into silence, his carefully constructed façade firmly in place. But slowly, painstakingly, cracks began to appear in his armour. He started to reveal more about his childhood, detailing instances of abuse and neglect that had shaped his worldview, his sense of self, and his profound need for control. These revelations weren't spontaneous confessions; they were meticulously extracted, gleaned from carefully worded questions, observations of his nonverbal cues, and subtle shifts in his demeanour.

When they emerged, the memories were fragmented, disjointed, and often shrouded in a haze of distortion and denial. But even these fragmented glimpses offered valuable insights into the genesis of his pathology. The repetitive patterns, the common themes of powerlessness, betrayal, and the overwhelming sense of being out of control—these elements underscored the deep-seated origins of his violent impulses. They revealed a man who, robbed of agency in his early years, had sought to reclaim it through the most horrific means imaginable.

The therapeutic process wasn't about offering a quick fix, a simple solution. It was a long and arduous journey into the depths of a troubled mind. My role was to guide him, help him navigate the treacherous terrain of his inner world, and confront the painful truths he had buried for so long. The ultimate goal wasn't just to understand his actions but to help him find a path towards healing, a path that led away from the abyss of violence and towards a fragile, but potentially possible, sense of peace. The road ahead was long and uncertain, but the first steps had been taken, and the initial cracks in his impenetrable fortress had begun to widen. The rain outside continued to fall, a relentless, mirroring rhythm, but inside the confines of my office, a subtle shift had begun.

The tempestuous narrative was slowly yielding to a more nuanced, more human story. And that, in itself, was a victory. A small, tentative triumph, but a victory nonetheless.

The initial breakthroughs were fragile, like shards of glass reflecting distorted images of his past. He'd speak of a childhood filled with chilling silences, punctuated by bursts of unpredictable rage from his father. The details were scarce, shrouded in a fog of repression and denial. Still, the underlying emotion—a profound sense of helplessness, of being utterly at the mercy of forces beyond his control—was palpable. He'd describe feeling invisible, like a ghost in his family home, his needs ignored and his cries for help unanswered. He spoke of being the silent observer of domestic violence, a constant witness to scenes of brutality and degradation that left an indelible mark on his young psyche.

These weren't confessions; they were fragments, glimpses into the abyss of his childhood trauma. Each memory was a jagged piece of a shattered puzzle, complex to assemble and even more challenging to interpret. The process felt akin to archaeological excavation, meticulously sifting through layers of denial and distortion to unearth the buried truths.

He would often stop mid-sentence, his eyes glazing over, a faraway look settling on his face. These lapses into silence were punctuated by sudden outbursts of anger, frustration, or even a surprising display of vulnerability, a tear tracing a path down his cheek, quickly wiped away as if it were a contaminant he couldn't allow himself to feel.

My approach was guided by principles of trauma-informed therapy, recognising the profound impact of his early experiences on his present state. The goal wasn't to extract details through forceful interrogation but to create a space where he felt safe enough to explore these painful memories at his own pace—I used narrative therapy techniques, encouraging him to tell his story in his own words, without judgment or interruption.

Focused on validating his emotions, helping him label and understand the long-buried and unacknowledged feelings. The sessions became a tapestry woven from fragments of memory and hesitant self-revelation. He began to speak of his attempts to regain control, to exert power in a world where he'd felt consistently powerless. His actions weren't merely acts of violence; they were desperate attempts to impose order on a chaotic inner world. The meticulous planning, the calculated execution, and the crafting of elaborate narratives were manifestations of his desperate need for control, a need born out of the profound sense of helplessness he experienced as a child.

We explored his cognitive distortions and how he manipulated information and perceptions to maintain a warped sense of self-worth. He believed his actions were justified, even necessary, to restore the balance he'd never had. His delusions of control were powerful, allowing him to create a false sense of order in a life that had felt consistently chaotic and unpredictable. We worked on challenging these distortions, gradually replacing them with more realistic and accurate perspectives.

The process was slow, painstaking, and filled with setbacks. There were times when he reverted to his usual detached demeanour, his carefully constructed defences firmly in place. He'd become sullen, withdrawn, refusing to engage in conversation, his eyes veiled with a chilling emptiness. At times, I doubted the effectiveness of the therapy, questioning if we were making any real progress. Those periods of stagnation served as a reminder of the enormity of the task. Recovery wasn't a linear path; it was a winding road with many twists and turns, ups and downs, and forward and backward movements.

But then, there were moments of progress, small glimmers of hope that kept us going. He started to acknowledge the impact of his actions on his victims, though not with remorse.

The acknowledgement itself was a landmark in his journey. He started to recognise the patterns of his behaviour, the self-destructive cycles that fuelled his violence. He began to see how his need for control had backfired, leading him into a more bottomless abyss of isolation and self-destruction.

In one session, he spoke about a recurring dream, a vivid nightmare in which he was a small child trapped in a dark room, crying out for help, his voice lost in the echoing silence. The dream, he said, represented his deepest fears—of powerlessness, abandonment, and the overwhelming sense of being alone. It was a breakthrough, a raw, unfiltered expression of his innermost traumas. This was not simply a clinical description but a visceral experience he finally allowed himself to confront.

As we delved deeper into his past, we explored the complex relationship between his childhood trauma and his present-day behaviour. We employed techniques like EMDR (Eye Movement Desensitisation and Reprocessing) to help him process the traumatic memories, mitigating their lingering impact. The EMDR sessions were challenging, bringing forth intense emotional reactions, vivid flashbacks, and unsettling sensations. But through the process, he gradually began to reframe his traumatic memories, diminishing their power and transforming their emotional impact.

Cognitive behavioural therapy (CBT) played a crucial role in helping him identify and modify his maladaptive thought patterns and behaviours. We worked on building coping mechanisms to manage his anger and impulse control, enabling him to recognise and manage situations before they escalated into violent outbursts. He began to see how his distorted thinking had justified his actions and how challenging those thoughts could lead to better choices.

The road to recovery was not solely focused on addressing the past. We also worked on building a more positive future. He explored his interests, aspirations, and untapped potential. He aimed to prevent future violence and cultivate a sense of purpose, self-worth, and genuine connection with the world. He was introduced to support groups, where he could connect with others with similar experiences, fostering a sense of community and shared understanding.

He began to engage in activities that fostered self-reflection and emotional regulation, such as meditation and mindfulness exercises. This was a crucial element of his recovery, as it made him more aware of his emotional state and better equipped to handle challenging situations. The introduction of art therapy was surprisingly effective. He began to express his emotions through painting and drawing, finding a non-verbal outlet for his thoughts and feelings. The artwork reflected a journey, progressing from dark and disturbing imagery to more hopeful and expressive pieces. It was a testament to his growing self-awareness and his capacity for healing.

The therapeutic process was not always smooth sailing. There were relapses, moments of intense resistance, and periods when his progress plateaued. But throughout these challenges, the focus remained on fostering hope, understanding, and resilience. Recovery was not a destination but an ongoing journey with many milestones and setbacks.

The ending of his therapy wasn't a dramatic climax; there

were no tearful confessions or sudden revelations. Instead, it was a gradual waning of his defensive structures, a softening of his rigid demeanour, and a tentative but discernible shift toward self-compassion. His gaze, which had once held a chilling emptiness, now carried a flicker of something else—vulnerability, perhaps, or a fragile hope for a different future. The journey was far from over, but he had begun to walk a path away from the darkness towards the uncertain yet hopeful light of healing. The road ahead would undoubtedly be challenging, filled with obstacles and hurdles. He now possessed a compass, a set of tools, and the strength of spirit, all forged in the crucible of his trauma and the long, arduous path to recovery. The rain outside had stopped.

CHAPTER 5
THE ALLEY'S SILENCE

he silence in the interrogation room was heavier than the humid summer air pressing against the barred window. It wasn't the oppressive silence of denial, the carefully constructed wall I'd erected for so long. This was different. This silence was the weight of my actions, the crushing burden of what I had done. It wasn't just the physical acts themselves—the violence, the calculated cruelty. It was the ripple effect, the devastation that spread outwards, shattering lives beyond repair. The faces of the victims, the anguish etched onto their features, flooded my memory—not as fleeting images, but as persistent, searing visions that burned themselves onto the back of my eyelids.I saw their families, their haunted eyes, their broken hearts. I heard their cries, their silent screams echoing in the empty spaces of my mind. And I listened to my voice for the first time—not the carefully constructed narrative I'd used to justify my actions, but a raw, desperate whisper of regret. It was a sound I'd never allowed myself to hear before, one that cut through the layers of denial and self-deception I'd painstakingly built.

The meticulously planned alibis, the fabricated stories, and the manipulation of evidence were all flimsy shields against the overwhelming truth. The truth was not just the legal definition of guilt but the moral weight of my transgressions, the profound sense of shame that settled heavily in my gut, a physical manifestation of the suffering I had inflicted. This wasn't remorse in the clinical sense; it was a visceral, gut-wrenching realisation of the damage I had caused. It wasn't a calculation, a strategic move to mitigate the consequences. It was an unyielding acceptance of responsibility that shook me to my core.

The acceptance wasn't a sudden epiphany, a dramatic shift from darkness to light. It was a gradual process, a slow dismantling of the intricate defence mechanisms that had protected me for so long. It was like peeling back layers of an onion, each layer revealing a deeper layer of pain, of guilt, of unacknowledged trauma. It was a painful process, exposing the raw nerve endings of my soul, leaving me vulnerable and exposed. But within that vulnerability, I found something I'd never allowed myself to feel before: empathy. I began to see the victims not as abstract entities or convenient targets but as individuals with lives, hopes, dreams, and families. I saw their pain, fear, and struggle not as obstacles in my path but as a direct result of my actions.

This empathy, this ability to connect with their suffering, was a terrifying yet liberating experience. It shattered the carefully constructed walls of my isolation, forcing me to confront the consequences of my choices. I began to understand the true meaning of responsibility—the profound weight of causing such immeasurable harm. The images of my victims' suffering were no longer merely a clinical description, a case study in forensic psychology. They were a haunting reminder of the human cost of my actions and the irreversible damage I had done.

The remorse wasn't a simple feeling; it was a complex tapestry of emotions—regret, shame, guilt, self-loathing, and profound sorrow. It wasn't something I could easily articulate; it was a visceral experience that resonated deeply. It was a weight that threatened to crush me, a burden I was finally willing to bear. I had spent so long running from it, shielding myself from its searing intensity, but I finally faced it head-on.

I wasn't seeking absolution; I was seeking to understand, atone, and find a way to reconcile with the darkness that had consumed me.

My acceptance wasn't a sign of weakness but a demonstration of strength. It acknowledged my flaws, capacity for evil, and profound need for redemption. It was a confession not only to the authorities but to myself—to the wounded parts of my soul that I had neglected for so long. The silence in the interrogation room now held a different quality, a profound sense of stillness that contrasted with the turmoil within. It was a silence born not of denial but of acceptance, a silence that carried the weight of my past and the faint whisper of hope for the future.

The path to redemption would be long and arduous, a constant battle against the insidious whispers of my inner demons. There would be days when the weight of my actions threatened to overwhelm me, memories would return with their searing intensity, and the ghosts of my past would haunt my every waking moment. But now, I have a different perspective and lens to view my past, present, and future. I would use this new understanding not as an excuse but as a catalyst for change.

This acceptance wasn't a simple acknowledgement of guilt; it was a radical transformation in my perception of myself, my past, and my role in the world. It was a dismantling of the carefully constructed narratives that had sustained my delusions of control. It was a shedding of the skin of the person I once was, a painful, protracted process of shedding the layers of denial, distortion, and self-deception that had protected me from the truth for so long.

The journey was far from over. The road ahead would be challenging, filled with obstacles and setbacks. There would be moments of despair, times when the weight of my actions would threaten to consume me. But now, I have the strength, resolve, and willingness to confront the darkness within and embark on the long and difficult journey towards healing and redemption.

I understood that true acceptance and remorse were not merely verbal acknowledgements; they were a deep-seated shift in my perspective, a fundamental change in how I viewed myself and my relationship with the world. This was a lifetime commitment, a relentless pursuit of self-improvement and atonement. It was not about seeking forgiveness from others but about finding forgiveness within myself, a journey that would require unwavering self-reflection, consistent self-improvement, and a steadfast commitment to making amends wherever possible. Accepting my condition wasn't simply a resignation from my past but a recognition of my inherent capacity for good and evil. I understood that my past actions were not an excuse for my behaviour but rather a window into the deep-seated psychological wounds that fueled my violence. This understanding didn't diminish the severity of my crimes but instead provided a context for comprehending the complex interplay of factors that contributed to my destructive behaviours.

This understanding would guide my future actions, informing my approach to therapy, my engagement with support groups, and my commitment to personal growth. The path to recovery wasn't about erasing the past but learning from it, using the lessons learned to build a more compassionate and responsible future. It was about transforming pain into purpose, using my experience to help others who had suffered similar traumas, to prevent others from travelling down the same dark path I had walked.

The path to redemption wasn't a straight line but a winding, often treacherous road filled with unexpected turns and steep inclines. It would require constant vigilance, ongoing introspection, and an unwavering commitment to self-improvement. But with each step forward, a moment of self-awareness, and an act of compassion, I would inch closer to a semblance of peace. Once a symbol of my isolation and detachment, the alley's silence had become a silent witness to my transformation. The silence was no longer empty; it was filled with the weight of my acceptance and the whisper of hope. The rain had stopped, and a pale sun peeked through the clouds, casting a sliver of light on the path ahead.The rain had stopped, but the damp chill clung to the alley, mirroring the persistent coldness that had settled in my bones. Once a comforting blanket of anonymity, the silence felt like a suffocating shroud. It wasn't the silence of emptiness but of unbearable weight and accumulated horrors. The alley seemed to hold its breath, a silent accomplice to the events unfolding within its shadowed walls.

My memories weren't like photographs, neatly filed and easily accessed. They were shards of glass, jagged and unpredictable, slicing through my consciousness at unexpected moments. A scent, a sound, a fleeting image could trigger a cascade of recollection, plunging me back into the heart of the darkness I had inhabited. I would see their faces again, not as hazy recollections, but as stark, vivid portraits etched into the recesses of my mind: the fear in their eyes, the desperate struggle, the final, agonising silence. These weren't just memories; they were living, breathing entities, haunting my every waking moment, whispering in the silence of the night.

The psychological impact was insidious, a slow, creeping poison that permeated every aspect of my being. Sleep offered no respite; instead, it became a battleground where nightmares raged, replaying the events with brutal, unforgiving detail. The waking hours were no better. The world around me seemed to warp and distort, the mundane becoming imbued with the macabre undercurrents of my past. Familiar places took on a sinister new meaning, their ordinary facades dissolving to reveal the darkness lurking beneath.

Even the simplest tasks became monumental struggles. Concentration evaporated, replaced by a fog of anxiety and guilt. The simplest conversations felt fraught with unspoken accusations, the slightest glance interpreted as judgment. Trust had become an alien concept, a luxury I no longer dared to afford. The world was a treacherous labyrinth, each turn revealing a new layer of suspicion, a new reminder of my transgressions.

My appetite vanished, replaced by a gnawing emptiness that mirrored the hollowness within. The physical manifestations were as alarming as the psychological ones. My hands trembled, my heart pounded incessantly, and my body reacted with involuntary spasms. I felt like a tightly wound spring, poised on the brink of snapping under the unrelenting pressure of my memories.

Therapy became a necessary, though often excruciating, ritual. Facing my past wasn't a matter of recounting events; it was a process of painstaking reconstruction, a meticulous examination of the events, my motivations, and the intricate web of psychological factors that had led me down this destructive path. My therapist, a patient and understanding woman with years of experience in treating trauma survivors, helped me navigate the treacherous terrain of my memories. She helped me understand the complex interplay of childhood trauma, personality disorders, and environmental influences that had shaped my actions.

The sessions were brutal, relentlessly peeling back the layers of self-deception and denial I had meticulously constructed over the years. The process was excruciating, but it was also liberating. With each revelation, each painful acknowledgement, I felt a glimmer of hope, a sense of moving forward, however slowly. But even with professional help, the burden of memory remained heavy, an unrelenting companion. The guilt was a constant, gnawing presence, a relentless inner voice that echoed the world's accusations. The shame was a crippling weight, crushing my self-esteem, leaving me feeling unworthy and irreparable. There were days when the despair was overwhelming when the memories would surge with such intensity that I would be incapacitated, overwhelmed by the sheer magnitude of my actions. In those days, the simple act of breathing felt like an immense struggle.

Yet, even in the darkest moments, a tenacious spark of hope remained, flickering like a candle in a storm. This hope wasn't based on wishful thinking or self-delusion; it was rooted in my growing understanding of my past, recognition of my responsibility, and capacity for empathy. I began to understand that my past was not a sentence but a challenge. It was an opportunity for growth, a chance to use my experiences to positively impact the world. The path to redemption was not a linear journey. It was a meandering path, fraught with setbacks and relapses. But with each small step, each moment of self-reflection, and each act of kindness,

I inched closer to a more compassionate understanding of myself and the world. I started volunteering at a local support group for victims of violence, sharing my story not as an excuse but as a warning, a cautionary tale about the destructive consequences of unchecked anger and unresolved trauma.

The work was challenging, deeply emotional, and sometimes incredibly difficult. I was forced to confront the pain and suffering I had inflicted on others to acknowledge the devastating impact of my actions. But with each act of empathy, each moment of connection, I began to heal. The process was not about seeking absolution; it was about acknowledging the unfathomable harm I had caused and working tirelessly to prevent others from experiencing similar pain.

The alley's silence, which once felt like a tomb, now felt different. It was no longer a symbol of isolation and despair but a testament to my journey of healing and redemption. The silence was a reminder of the past, yes. Still, it was also a canvas upon which I painted a new future built on self-awareness, compassion, and the unwavering determination to use my experience to help others. The rain had stopped, and the sun, though pale, shone through the clouds, casting a ray of hope upon the long, arduous journey ahead. The journey was far from over, but for the first time, I could see a glimmer of light at the end of the tunnel. The silence wasn't just an absence of sound; it was the pregnant pause before the next chapter, filled with the possibility of healing, growth, and redemption. The burden of memory remained, but it no longer crushed me. I carried it, yes, but I carried it with a newfound strength, a quiet resolve, and the unwavering belief that even from the deepest darkness, a path to light could be found.

The weight of my past didn't lessen overnight; it was a gradual, painstaking process akin to lifting a mountain one grain of sand at a time. The alley, once a symbol of my deepest shame, now became a place of quiet contemplation. I would return, not to relive the horrors, but to confront them, to acknowledge their presence without succumbing to their power. The silence, once suffocating, now felt like a space for reflection, a sanctuary where I could commune with my own thoughts, unburdened by the cacophony of judgment. My therapist suggested volunteering, a suggestion that initially filled me with trepidation. How could I, a perpetrator, possibly help victims? The very thought felt like a grotesque mockery, a cruel irony. But she insisted that true redemption wasn't about erasing the past but actively working to prevent future harm. It was about transforming the destructive energy that consumed me into something constructive and positive. I began volunteering at a local shelter for women escaping domestic violence. The initial encounters were excruciating. The women's stories, their pain, their resilience—a relentless torrent of emotion that threatened to overwhelm me. I saw reflections of myself.

In their eyes—the fear, the helplessness, the desperate yearning for escape. The guilt intensified, a sharp, stabbing pain that pierced through my carefully constructed defences. There were days when I wanted to flee, to retreat back into the suffocating cocoon of my own self-loathing.

But I persevered. I listened, I empathised, and I offered whatever support I could. I learned to channel my own experiences not as excuses but as tools. I understood the nuances of manipulation and the insidious ways abusers exploit their victims' vulnerabilities. My knowledge of psychology, once a tool for destruction, became a weapon for empowerment. I helped them navigate the legal system, provided emotional support, and created safety plans.

The work was emotionally draining but also profoundly fulfilling. Witnessing these women's transformation, their journey from despair to hope, gave me a sense of purpose, a reason to keep going. It wasn't about seeking forgiveness; it was about making amends and proving to myself and the world that I was capable of change.

I started small, offering practical help—driving women to appointments, assisting with paperwork, and providing a listening ear. Gradually, I built trust, and the women began sharing their stories with me. Their vulnerability, courage, and unwavering strength in the face of unimaginable adversity—a lesson in resilience that I desperately needed. I saw their struggle as my reflection and began understanding empathy's true meaning. It wasn't about feeling sorry for them but about understanding their pain, fears, and hopes on a deep, visceral level.

I found myself reaching out to organisations dedicated to mental health awareness. I initially shared my story anonymously, hesitant to expose myself to the potential backlash. But the responses were overwhelmingly positive. People shared their own experiences, and I realised that my story wasn't unique; it was a testament to the pervasive nature of trauma and the importance of seeking help.

I began to speak publicly, my voice trembling at first, then gaining strength with each shared experience. I talked about the insidious nature of untreated mental illness, the devastating consequences of unchecked anger, and the importance of early intervention and ongoing support. I became an advocate for mental health, a beacon of hope for others struggling in the darkness.

The process was far from easy. There were setbacks, moments of doubt, and times when the weight of my past threatened to overwhelm me. Some people refused to forgive me and saw my efforts as a mere act of self-preservation, a desperate attempt to alleviate my own guilt. Their scepticism stung, but I refused to let it derail my journey. I understood that redemption wasn't about winning their approval; it was about aligning my actions with my values, about living a life that reflected the changes I had made within myself.

While volunteering at the shelter one evening, I encountered a young woman who reminded me so much of myself. She was withdrawn and fearful, her eyes reflecting the pain she had endured. As I listened to her story, I saw my reflection in her words. Her trauma, though different, resonated deeply with my own experiences. My empathy for her was overwhelming, a profound connection that transcended the boundaries of our experiences. At that moment, I understood the true meaning of redemption – not as absolution but as a lifelong commitment to making amends, helping others find their way out of the darkness, and constantly striving to become a better version of myself. The alley still held its secrets, but its silence no longer held me captive. The silence had become a space for reflection, gratitude, and hope. It was a testament to the resilience of the human spirit, the enduring power of empathy, and the unwavering belief in the possibility of redemption, however arduous the path might be. The journey continued, but I walked it with a newfound sense of purpose and a quiet determination to use my experiences to make a meaningful difference in the lives of others. The rain had stopped, and the sun shone brightly, casting a warm glow on the path ahead. The future wasn't without its challenges, but I was ready to face them, not with fear, but with hope and unwavering resolve.

The path to redemption wasn't a straight line but a winding road full of twists and turns, setbacks and breakthroughs. There were days when the darkness threatened to engulf me once more when the weight of my past felt insurmountable. But I learned to navigate these treacherous terrains, to find solace in the quiet moments of reflection, to draw strength from the support of others, and to find purpose in helping those who were still struggling in the darkness. Each act of service, each conversation, and each moment of connection served as a reminder of my commitment to change, a testament to the power of empathy, and a beacon of hope in the ongoing journey toward a more compassionate and meaningful life.

My story wasn't just a tale of redemption; it was a story of transformation, a testament to the resilience of the human spirit, and a reminder that even from the deepest darkness, a path to healing and a brighter future can be found. The alley's silence, once a haunting reminder of my past, had transformed into a sanctuary, a place where I could reflect on my journey, celebrate my progress, and renew my commitment to a life dedicated to service, compassion, and the unwavering pursuit of a more meaningful existence. The journey toward redemption was far from over, but with each step, I walked closer towards the light, guided by the unwavering belief that even the darkest of nights must eventually give way to the dawn. The silence was not an ending but a pregnant pause, a moment of reflection before the next chapter, a chapter filled with the promise of hope, healing, and a future dedicated to making amends and inspiring others to find their own paths towards redemption. The quiet hum of the city, a stark contrast to the oppressive silence of the alley, became a comforting soundtrack to my newfound routine. I was drawn to the vibrant energy of the streets, a world away from the shadows that had once consumed me. The faces I encountered, a kaleidoscope of expressions, no longer triggered the same fear and self-loathing. Instead, I saw stories of struggle, resilience, and hope. Each interaction became a small victory, a testament to my evolving ability to connect with others on a human level without the suffocating weight of my past dragging me down. My work at the shelter wasn't without its challenges. The emotional toll was immense; there were days when the weight of others' suffering felt almost unbearable. I'd retreat to the quiet sanctuary of my apartment, allowing myself to feel the raw grief and despair that threatened to overwhelm me. But I no longer saw these moments as failures, evidence of weakness. They were opportunities for self-reflection and processing the complex emotions that arose from bearing witness to the pain of others. I learned to recognise the boundaries of my capacity for empathy, learning to prioritise my well-being without compromising my commitment to helping others. Self-care was no longer an indulgence but a necessary component of my healing.

I discovered the power of mindfulness, learning to ground myself in the present moment to appreciate life's small joys and simple pleasures. I began practising yoga, finding solace in the physicality of the poses, the calming breathwork, and the quiet introspection it fostered. The practice helped me cultivate a sense of body awareness, a connection to myself that had been severed for so long. It helped me manage the lingering anxiety and the intrusive thoughts that occasionally crept into my consciousness. The physical practice became a metaphor for my emotional journey: a slow, steady process of stretching, strengthening, and, ultimately, finding a new sense of balance and stability.

My relationships with others also evolved. The initial hesitancy and fear of intimacy gradually led to trust and genuine connection. I found myself drawn to people who were compassionate, empathetic, and willing to engage in honest self-reflection.

I learned the importance of setting boundaries and protecting my emotional well-being without compromising my ability to connect with others. These relationships, built on mutual respect and understanding, became sources of strength and support, reminding me that I was not alone on my journey.

The anonymity that had shielded me during my early public speaking engagements eventually faded. I felt a growing sense of responsibility to share my story openly and honestly and to use my experience to challenge the stigma surrounding mental illness and trauma. It was a daunting decision, fraught with fear and uncertainty. The possibility of rejection, judgment, and facing the consequences of my past actions loomed large. But the desire to make a difference, to inspire hope in others, outweighed my fears.

I began writing, transforming my experiences into a narrative that resonated with the complexities of human nature. The words flowed, a cathartic release of emotions that had long been suppressed. Writing became a form of self-therapy, a way to process my emotions, make sense of my past, and forge a path toward healing. I found a community of writers who understood the power of storytelling as a tool for healing and social change.

Their encouragement and support became invaluable as I navigated the challenges of sharing my vulnerabilities with the world.

The publication of my work was a watershed moment. The responses were varied—some were filled with empathy and understanding, others with scepticism and judgment. But the positive feedback far outweighed the negative, a testament to the power of honest self-reflection and the growing acceptance of mental health issues. Sharing my story provided a voice for others who had struggled in silence, a reminder that they were not alone and that healing was possible. My journey continues, and it is far from linear. The shadows of the past still linger, but they no longer hold me captive. I've learned to coexist with them, to acknowledge their presence without being consumed by their power. Once a symbol of shame and despair, the alley holds a different significance. It serves as a reminder of my past and a testament to my resilience and capacity for growth and change. It is a place where I can reflect on the path I've travelled, the challenges I've overcome, and the hope that guides me forward.

The scars remain visible reminders of the pain and suffering I endured. But these scars are not badges of shame; they are symbols of my resilience, strength, and capacity for transformation. They are a testament to the power of the human spirit to overcome adversity, find meaning in suffering, and emerge from the darkness into the light. The healing process is ongoing, a lifelong commitment to self-awareness, self-compassion, and continuous growth.

The future remains uncertain, but I approach it with purpose and determination. My past will always be a part of me, but it will no longer define me. I am committed to using my experiences to help others, advocate for mental health awareness, and inspire hope in struggling people. The journey toward redemption has been arduous, but it has been profoundly transformative. I have learned the invaluable lessons of empathy, resilience, and the enduring power of the human spirit to heal, grow, and find meaning even in the darkest times. The silence of the alley has become a sanctuary, a place of quiet contemplation and reflection, where I can connect with my inner self, draw strength from my experiences, and renew my commitment to a life of service, compassion, and unwavering hope. The sun continues to rise, casting a warm glow on the path ahead, illuminating the way toward a brighter, more meaningful future. And I walk that path, not with fear, but with a quiet determination, guided by the unwavering belief in the possibility of healing and redemption.

The silence of the alley, once a suffocating blanket of shame and despair, now resonates with a different kind of quiet. It's the quiet of acceptance and understanding, the quiet that comes after the storm. Once stained with the residue of my darkest hours, the bricks now witness a different narrative of resilience, healing, and the slow, arduous climb out of the abyss.

Looking back, I see the alley not as a place of isolation but as a crucible where my fractured self was forged anew. Once a terrifying and uncontrollable force, the darkness within me now exists as a companion. This shadow reminds me of the fragility of thehuman condition and the constant need for vigilance and self-care. It's a reminder that the battle for mental health is a lifelong journey, not a destination.

There's no final victory, no declaration of complete and utter triumph. It's a daily practice, constant recalibration, and continuous negotiation with the demons lurking within. The path to recovery wasn't linear. There were setbacks and moments of profound despair where the shadows threatened to engulf me again. But each time, I found the strength to fight back, to claw my way back to the light. The support system I had painstakingly built — the friends, the therapists, the support groups — became my lifeline, a network of individuals who understood the complexities of mental illness and the challenges of recovery. They provided the scaffolding I needed to rebuild my life, brick by brick, moment by moment.

My work with the shelter became a pivotal part of my healing journey. Helping others navigate their struggles and offering a hand to those stumbling in the darkness provided a profound sense of purpose and meaning. It allowed me to channel my pain into something positive and transform my suffering into a source of strength and empathy. Witnessing the resilience of others and their capacity to overcome adversity reinforced my belief in the power of the human spirit to heal and transform.

The publication of my memoir brought a different set of challenges. The public exposure was daunting, the vulnerability terrifying. The fear of judgment, rejection, and being misunderstood was palpable. But I pressed on, driven by the desire to break down the stigma surrounding mental health and to provide a voice for those who had suffered in silence. The responses were varied, a kaleidoscope of emotions mirroring the complexities of human nature. Some offered unwavering support, empathy, and understanding. Others remained skeptical, judgmental, and even hostile. But the outpouring of positive feedback — the messages of hope and gratitude from those who felt seen and heard — reinforced the importance of sharing my story.

The healing process isn't about erasing the past or pretending it never happened. It's about acknowledging the pain, integrating the trauma, and learning to live with the scars. These visible and invisible scars are no blemishes to be hidden or ashamed of. They are badges of honor, testaments to the battles fought and won. They are reminders of the strength I've found within myself, the resilience I've cultivated, and the lessons I've learned along the way.

My story is not unique. Millions struggle with mental illness, facing stigma, discrimination, and a lack of access to adequate care. My hope is that my experience will inspire others to seek help, break the silence, and confront the darkness within. The fight for mental health equality is far from over. We need to advocate for increased funding for mental healthcare, for the development of innovative treatment approaches, and for the dismantling of the stigma that perpetuates suffering.

The alley's legacy is not one of despair and hopelessness. It's a legacy of transformation, a testament to the power of the human spirit to overcome adversity and find meaning even in the darkest times. It's a reminder that healing is possible, recovery is achievable, and hope, however fragile, can endure even in the face of overwhelming despair. The silence of the alley, once a symbol of my struggles, now represents a quiet strength, a quiet resilience, and a quiet hope for the future. The journey continues — the work and the struggle are ongoing. The shadows remain, but they no longer control me. I have learned to live with them, understand them, and integrate them into the tapestry of my being. I am a work in progress, constantly evolving and learning, and clearly, shelter work, writing, and connections have been pivotal elements in my journey toward wholeness.

My purpose now is to use my experiences to help others, advocate for mental health awareness, challenge stigma, and provide a beacon of hope for struggling people. The alley's legacy is not simply my redemption; it's a call to action, a plea for empathy, a demand for better mental healthcare systems that support and empower those in need. It's a reminder that mental illness is not a character flaw; it's a medical condition that requires understanding, compassion, and effective treatment.

We need to create a world where individuals struggling with mental illness are not ostracized, marginalized, or left to suffer in silence. We need to cultivate a culture of compassion and understanding, where seeking help is not a sign of weakness but a sign of strength. We must invest in comprehensive mental healthcare systems, ensuring equitable access to quality care for all, regardless of socioeconomic status or geographic location. We need to train healthcare professionals, educators, and community leaders to recognize the signs and symptoms of mental illness and to respond with empathy and understanding.

The silence of the alley has given way to a chorus of voices — the voices of those who have found their way back from the brink, those who are fighting for their lives, the voices of those who refuse to let the darkness define them. This is a story of individual healing, collective action, societal change, and a future where mental health is prioritized, valued, and understood. The alley's legacy is not an ending; it is a beginning. The beginning of a movement towards a more compassionate, understanding, and supportive world — a world where mental health is not a taboo but a topic of open conversation and proactive intervention. A world where the resounding voice of hope, resilience, and recovery replaces the silence of the alley. And in that hope, I find my peace, purpose, and strength to continue walking forward. The sun, after all, does rise every single day.